Johnson County Public Library
401 South State Street
Franklin, IN 46131

9/10 (15) 9/08

MIGHTY BIG RIVER

Two families: the Arlens—Libby, her husband Alister, and five youngsters; and the Biggers—Sarah and Mose with their uncountable brood.

And one man—a gentle giant named Matt Cowan.

They had just 29 days to get to the Willamette Valley in time to stake out claims for free land. The only way to even get close to that was to travel the lot of them down the swollen Columbia River on open rafts.

They all knew that some would not make it . . .

MIGHTY BIG RIVER

Chad Merriman

This hardback edition 1999
by Chivers Press
by arrangement with
Golden West Literary Agency

ISBN 0 7540 8071 4

British Library Cataloguing in Publication Data available

Printed and bound in Great Britain by
Redwood Books, Trowbridge, Wiltshire

Chapter 1

It was the gentle giant who nearly unnerved Libby that last morning. He was Matt Cowan, a horse-backer who had thrown in with the straggling wagons somewhere west of Fort Hall. He had no family to fear for, and the strength of two ordinary men. If he could have kept the worry out of his own eyes that morning, she might have been spared the fear tying knots in her stomach.

But he kept looking at the troubled river and off toward the mist-blurred gorge and up at the mountains where in the night they could see that snow had fallen. The river gorge went like a knife-cut through the mountains, but the cattle could not be taken down by raft, so Matt Cowan would drive them over those mountains. The prospect sobered him that morning and did worse than that to her, for her ten-year-old Win would go along to help him, as would Dob Biggers who was only two years older.

Dob stayed with the cattle: the sorefooted oxen that had pulled the two dish-wheeled wagons all the way from the Missouri, and the milk cows both families were taking to the valley beyond the mountains. But Matt Cowan turned away from them and brought Win to the fire where Libby and Sarah Biggers sat with their smaller children. He addressed himself to Libby, for Sarah Biggers showed no more anxiety over their situation than she had over the other bad stretches on the trail, although this was the worst of them all.

"Reckon we'll get started, Miz Arlen." Matt Cowan's voice was deep, bell-toned, yet as gentle as his gray eyes. There wasn't an ounce of fat on him, or of showy muscle. He was fashioned like any other man, only hugely. "We ought to be waitin' for you at the crossing a couple of days from now."

"I'm sure you will be." Libby's breath was short, her heart tripping, because he would have a part of her life in his hands until then. She couldn't help voicing her concern and added hesitantly, "I—hope you don't run into too much snow up there."

Sarah Biggers cut off his reply with a short laugh. "What have they got to worry about? If they get snowed in up there they got plenty of beef along. We're the ones, if we get hung up, that'll go empty."

Matt Cowan's eyes shifted to her and for a moment weren't quite so gentle. He didn't answer her. Libby could have done so with pleasure, for the Biggerses were about as improvident a family as it had been her misfortune to meet, much less to be thrown with so closely out of necessity. But instead of shooting off her face as she had been itching to do for days, she looked at her son and her breath caught. He was so small for what he had to do, and she wanted to take him in her arms and hold him. But he would hate that and it might be her own complete undoing.

She said, as a mother ought to, "Now, you mind Mister Cowan. He's the boss till you see us again. You hear?"

"Yes, Mamma."

In his blond slightness he was the spit and image of his father. She couldn't say any more and smiled at him. He smiled back uncertainly, then turned, and he and Matt Cowan went striding off toward the waiting cattle. She turned back to the fire and her other four children, who sat solemnly with Sarah and the eight-year-old Amy Biggers. The girl, as pretty as her own Letty, was the only one in that family without the look of shiftlessness to her.

Sarah Biggers said with the placidity of the obtuse, "Don't fret so, Miz Arlen. They got to learn to look out for theirselves."

"I know that."

The little band of cattle was moving westward across the flat toward the snow-powdered mountains. Dob Biggers was chucking rocks at them, while Matt Cowan walked behind, leading his horse which now was packed with their camp. Win was on the near side and looked so small and alone with people almost strangers that she wanted to call and stop him. Yet she only watched until he looked toward her guardedly. She waved and he grinned and lifted his small hand, and the brush and rocks began to swallow them.

Not wanting to watch them disappear altogether, Libby looked down toward the river where Alister, Mose Biggers and the nineteen year-old Toby Biggers were putting the last of their possessions aboard the raft. Or rather where Alister and Toby were doing so, with the gaunt, whiskery Mose mostly watching and offering advice. He was a drone and a leech, and she would have given anything if breakdown after breakdown hadn't teamed up the two wagons perforce and thrown them so far behind the big trains where there was help and safety and a chance for a body to choose his own company.

The raft, made of forty-foot logs the men had cut and dragged to the river to be lashed together, was weighted so that its deck was only a few inches higher than the water even without the passengers on it. The beds of the knocked-down wagons made deckhouses fore and aft that would be their only shelter once they cast off. It seemed too frail a vessel to be trusted with their possessions and lives. The Cascades were forty miles downstream, a day's rafting beyond the cattle crossing. They were the immediate objective for there was a store there, but they were still within the gorge and hardly more than halfway to the Willamette Valley and the free land they had come to claim.

The men were about through with the last loading and lashing down, and Alister looked so thin and so much older now than his thirty years. Yet, while she hadn't looked in a mirror for weeks, she had no doubt that she looked well past her own twenty-eight. She had always been small and slight, but Alister had been twenty pounds heavier when they left Missouri in late spring.

Not wanting to think of the toll the venture that once had seemed so promising and easy had taken and might take still, Libby glanced off up the river. This great, rocky flat ran in that direction to the village grown up around Fort Dalles, a dozen or so cabins and a small store. At some distance were the Indian villages formed about the missions of the Catholics and Methodists. On beyond, an enormous bald headland brought a spur of the mountains curving back to touch the river, creating this pocket called The Dalles.

And then she looked at the river up there, leaden in the morning and split by jagged rock islands. Channels of surging water roared between the black rocks which the French trappers had named the *dalles* because they were like a giant's stepping-stones. To Libby they represented the ferocity of this biggest river she had ever seen and, shuddering, she brought her inspection back to camp by letting it travel along the mountains hugging the river on the far shore.

The cattle band had wholly vanished into the rocks and growth. Alister, she saw, was coming toward the fire while Mose Biggers and Toby kept fiddling around the raft. Libby's eyes rested on the sire of the brood, whom she could tolerate the least of them all, while she rememberd Sarah Biggers' complaint that it was the raft party that stood to go hungry if something went wrong to hold them up. As surely things had, one after the other, back along the trail. She knew that Sarah had run out of flour and coffee back on the Malheur and that the family had lived since then on a deadly diet of bacon and beans.

Even Alister had prodded Mose Biggers about reprovisioning at the store at the fort before they went on. She remembered the devil-may-care way the man had brushed it aside. "Pshaw, Mister Arlen, it's hardly a skip and a jump now to the valley, and we got vittles to see us through. Money's scarcer'n hens' teeth out there, I hear, and till we start gettin' it raised we got to buy what we eat. So if you took *my* advice, you'd hold onto your'n." Mose Biggers

MIGHTY BIG RIVER 9

was as full of foolish counsel as he was of contrariness and something else Libby had come to suspect. Stinginess, except when it came to himself. She knew he had spent money to buy himself the tobacco that kept his lips stained from morning to night and, from the state he had been in a couple of days, whiskey as well.

Alister was smiling as he came toward them, but his handsome lean face was somber. He was too tired, for he had neither the vast power of Matt Cowan nor the stringy toughness of the adult Biggers males. Nor their experience with hard muscular labor, she added to herself with pride. He had studied the law and meant to practice it when they reached their destination and had filed on their free land. It would keep them going until the farm started paying and afterward would help him in politics, perhaps to become a new state's governor.

Sarah had climbed to her feet, as had Amy. Neither looked nervous, and Libby wondered if this was because they lacked the imagination to be frightened. Her own little ones scrambled up, energized by the approach of their father. Letty eight, John six, Margaret four, Pip two. Alister said he had known what he was doing when he fathered them at such exact intervals. It made it easier to keep track of their ages. Libby stood up, although her knees were weak and trembling.

Alister's smile warmed as they met, and as always it made Libby's heart turn over. Not only because he was an attractive man whose love was as sure as the river's flowing. They hadn't been able to be man and wife for so long because of the cooped-up living and later the weariness, and she missed it as much as he did for she was a responsive woman.

She had purposely let Sarah Biggers move out of earshot with Amy. Now she managed to return Alister's smile and say under her breath, "Well. Did you finally get the thing loaded to the admiral's satisfaction?"

He grinned at her. "Don't let him get under your skin so, Libby. He's a nuisance sometimes, but he means well."

Libby wasn't so sure of that, and she was less sure of the younger Biggers who was silent and sullen ordinarily but given to watching her with sly, secretive eyes that frightened as well as annoyed her. She said, "I wish we could have kept Win with us and sent that Toby with the cattle."

"I know. But they said at the fort it takes three grown men to handle a raft on this river. Win'll be all right. He's a gritty little chap, and Cowan's the right sort."

"Thank heaven for that." Libby knew Matt Cowan would lay down his life to protect the boys with him, not understanding why she was so sure but just the same certain. "Oh, Alister. Are you sure we'll get there in time?"

"Positive. We ought to have at least three weeks to find our land."

That was a matter that had worried them more than they had admitted to each other or could admit even yet. They had to be in the valley by December first, just twenty nine days more. On that date the law that allowed land claims of six hundred and forty acres to a married man would run out, after which it would be possible to file on only half that much. They needed the maximum the way the babies kept coming, although it didn't look like the one due this year by Alister's plan would even get started.

And would three weeks be long enough to find their land? Libby's heart, as it had all morning, began to sink. For some eight years now the great trains of wagons had rolled out to the Willamette, bringing thousands upon thousands of land seekers as longing and needful as themselves. She didn't have to ponder long to realize how this must have filled up the country, making good land scarce and hard to find. And they would be on the tail end of it, the same as they had been the last in so much else on the way to the West.

Libby was filled with instant guilt by this mild complaint. It wasn't Alister's fault, having had seven mouths to feed from a poor practice, that there had been so little money. Yet she couldn't help thinking how, had there been enough, the way would have been smoothed out for them. With a good outfit they could have reached the Columbia while the steamboat, the *Flint*, was still coming up from The Cascades with supplies and taking back emigrants who could afford the passage. Or they could have taken the toll road south and over the mountains that now was closed to all but the most hardy and foolhardy. But thousands of others had rafted the gorge, and so could the Arlens with the dubious help of the Biggerses.

Yet Libby experienced some doubt of this when she followed Alister and the little ones over the gangplank onto the unsteady raft. Just that short distance, and the river became twice as wide and swift, the misty walls of the gorge they must enter twice as high and confining, her family twice as vulnerable. The Biggers wagon was the hind one, and Sarah was settling herself there with Amy. Resigned, patient, obtuse. Momentarily Libby envied the lank, slatternly woman her stoicism.

Pole in hand, Mose Biggers stood at the front of the raft, prepared to stave off rocks, Indians or buffalo stampedes, the need arising. He was a bald man under his floppy black hat, but he made up for it with whiskers colored by the gray of his years and tobacco. He grinned at her, saying cheerily, "You're lookin' a mite pale at the gills, Miz Arlen. Don't you fret now. We'll have us there in jig time."

"Just you get us there alive," Libby said tartly.

She turned to Alister, who had helped the children into the forward wagon box and under its dome of flapping, weathered canvas. The front flap was tied back, and he said, "Why don't you sit on the seat where you can watch the scenery? This is said to be the scenic spot of America, not barring the palisades of the Hudson."

Libby wrinkled her nose, for she had never seen water in such ill-humored immensity. Yet she dared not quail at the outset or she would be a quaking lump at the finish. So she let him help her into the seat and tuck a blanket over her lap.

"Cleopatra descending the Nile in her royal barge," he said, grinning at her. "Except she wasn't half as beautiful."

"Or half as scared."

"Can't say I blame you, Libby. It's a mighty big river."

He kissed her and went back to help cast off, and all too soon the raft seemed to shiver, then edge out timidly into the dark brown water. The men poled it offshore until the current caught, and then the stern sweep cut them sharply out from the bank. Away from the sheltering land the wind blew twice as hard and flapped and snapped the canvas. Libby looked down at her knotted hands, loosened them and glanced back at the children. They were all round-eyed although they could see nothing but each other, and the stuff still in the wagon box and the slatting canvas. Two, four, six and eight, with ten now somewhere on the snowy mountains above them. She fought down a sudden alarm and brought her head back deliberately to look forward.

The Columbia at first ran almost north, after which she knew it would make a gradual curve to the west. A high point of land on the left shore pushed hard against the river. It had become a familiar sight from their camp and was called Crate's Point because of a nearby settler. As they came around it she saw that the mountain hugging the right bank changed to perpendicular walls of lava rock. She had heard about these, too, and knew they were called the Paha Cliffs which the Indians said their coyote god had created by turning mortals and beasts into stone pillars. She mused on all this, but it didn't keep her from noticing how badly the raft yawed and pitched. How combers like those of an ocean surf ran whitely ahead. How low the mists now hung above the tormented water.

She shut her eyes, and almost at once a male voice said with a kind of cackle, "That won't make it all go 'way, Miz Arlen." She opened them, and there was Toby who had worked his way forward. He grinned at her in the way he had when none of the older ones were near, an aggressive, prying, suggestive smirk. It infuriated her, for to her mind he had only succeeded in combining the worst features of his father and mother. She supposed Alister was at the sweep, it being the hardest job, and didn't know what Mose Biggers was doing. But she had to dominate this lecherous fellow herself, or sooner or later he would give her serious trouble.

"You seem to think you're an improvement," she said coldly, "but you're wrong."

He gawked, cackled again and vanished.

The children all sat bundled to the ears where their father had placed them. All at once Libby wondered if the pitching would make them seasick and said anxiously, "Darlings, are you all right?" They nodded their heads: Letty, John, Margaret, Pip. They would all grow up in Oregon and become leaders, she mused, even the girls for they were as smart as the boys. Just three days to The Cascades, two more to Willamette, and it would be all over, with this experience something that in later years she would like to tell about.

"We were so poor we had only a dish-wheeled wagon, and we came to the Columbia so late and strapped what we had to a raft. But we made it fine, and then we found this wonderful land and never drew another uneasy breath. . . ."

Chapter 2

They still had the cliffs on the right, while on the south shore a mountain pushed up into the overcast and disappeared. As Libby watched the changing lower shapes of this she realized that the raft was moving in closer to it. For a moment this alarmed her, for offshore rocks dotted the forward distance as far as she could see. Then she understood that the men had decided to steer them into slacker water, and while this slowed them the raft rode more quietly there. Yet the wind was every bit as strong, and this brought Alister up to where she sat.

"Got to batten you in," he explained, trying to sound light about it. "You're scooping so much wind it holds us back."

"Does it always blow this hard?" she asked.

"Well, it always blows, I hear," Alister said, letting down the flaps. "Upstream or down. In winter it's mostly a west wind, which means a headwind for us. But it's not steady, they say, so if it doesn't slack off pretty soon we'll tie up and wait till it does."

Libby would almost welcome that, although they could ill afford the lost time. She crawled over the back of the seat and joined the children while Alister tied them in against the awesome outdoors. The young ones seemed grateful to have her closer, and she laughed and talked with them. The canvases slatted and cracked, and a little

14

later it started to rain. Soon rain was drumming on the canvas, with some of it blowing in.

She lost track of time and knew that midday had come only when Alister stuck his head through the back flaps and said they should eat. Feeling for the first time that she had a useful place in the weird world they had entered, Libby got to her knees, opened the kitchen box, and gave him two split biscuits with fried bacon laid between.

"How far have we come?" she asked.

"Well—" His eyes left hers. "It's hard to tell."

"That means not far," she said.

He said nothing and looked so drenched and frozen she was ashamed of her complaint, but he withdrew his head before she could make amends. She gave food to the children, and they ate hungrily, but she had no appetite. Afterward she got the younger ones to nap through an afternoon that brought no lull in the wind and rain. She persuaded Letty to lie down and shut her eyes, but at eight Letty could sense that they had moved into dangers more grimly imminent than they had estimated at The Dalles. Libby sat watching her quiet yet uneasy face, thinking how pretty she was, how well-built and how she would one day grow into a splendid woman.

And then she sat waiting until, if the time ever came, they made land. Yet her blinded sense of motion had grown so confused she didn't know that the raft had nosed into the bank and was only bobbing up and down, until Alister unfastened the back canvas.

He started to be gay about it, then saw how miserable they were and said quietly, gently, "We'll have a big fire in a minute, then a piping hot supper, and everybody will feel better."

"Alister," Libby said in a hushed voice. "Let's camp apart."

"We can't, Libby. On the trail it was the custom. But it would be too pointed now."

He helped her over the tailgate and afterward held her a moment with a wet arm across her shoulders, trying to tell her that he yearned for privacy as much as she did. It was still raining but not quite so hard. While they had pulled in on the lee of a huge pinacle, the wind that whipped around it reached them and was colder than it had been all day.

"You must be miserable," she whispered. "And me with my petty complaints."

He smiled, tightened his arm, then released her. Libby looked about and saw that they were on a flat shore on the river's south side. It was treeless, yet there was scads of driftwood, which must have persuaded the men to tie up there to make camp. Mose and Toby Biggers were already gathering wood, although Libby told herself it was only the thought of a comfortable fire that made them so industrious. She lifted her eyes, but the mountain that rose not far away was dissolved in the weeping clouds. And so was Win, but she wouldn't let herself picture him up there, somewhere, with virtual strangers.

Sarah Biggers came around the back end of the other wagon box, her unfeeling expression unchanged. Libby helped the children out of their own shelter, then herded them ashore. Oddly, she had so accommodated herself to the raft that now the earth seemed unsteady. She looked back to watch Alister carry the kitchen box off the raft. Toby brought up an armload of drift and dumped it. He gave her his sly grin, then answered his mother's call and went onto the raft to carry off their shabby equipage. Mose came in with wood, whittled shavings, and started a fire. She conceded that he was good at that, at least. The children hovered about, hungry, shivering and, Libby was sure, scared half to death of the wild place and the impending night.

She hoped wanly that Alister would change his mind and make them a separate fire. He failed to do so, and she tried to persuade herself that his attitude was proper, her own selfish and snobbish. Yet the unfairness of it stuck in her craw for they would have to share the food, her own carefully husbanded larder pooled with the Biggerses' skimpy supplies. For she wouldn't hold back from her own family and match their bacon and beans in kind.

So she found herself cooking supper with Sarah while the men put up a fly to keep off the rain. It was the look on Amy's face, when food odors began to spread, that made her feel better, yet she nearly lost her grip on her charity when she heard Mose say gustily, "Man, smell that there coffee." She made herself remember that he and Toby had been out in the cutting wind all day, the same as Alister.

She had the makings for biscuits that baked in the Dutch oven, and she had potatoes and dried onions to flavor and enrich the soup she suggested making from Sarah's bacon and beans. It had been her practice to cook enough at night to provide a quick breakfast, which she would not have done that night if she had foreseen the way the other family would pitch into it. When the meal was over there was nothing left for the next morning, and Libby's pleasure as a cook wasn't heightened when Mose belched noisily.

And while she grew more and more depressed, the food and warmth heightened his sense of well-being. "Wal, we din't do so good today," he admitted, biting off a chew of tobacco. "But tomorrow this wind'll be down, and we'll go hell a-kitin'. You mark my word."

"We better," Sarah said with less conviction, "if we're gonna get any land to live on. A powerful lot of people got there afore us."

"We'll get her. Land's what we come for, and I'll get mine or know what."

You sure will, Libby agreed.

She felt no better when, later, she had a degree of privacy in their wagon bed. Alister's exhaustion disclosed itself in the way he fell asleep almost before the children did. But Libby knew she couldn't sleep, for the wind by then was howling up the gorge. Its tone rose to shrieks wherever it split on some sharp edge, and waves rolled under them until the raft pitched crazily.

She had wanted to talk to Alister once the children were asleep. She hesitated about waking him. But she simply couldn't contain herself so, nudging him, she whispered, "Alister?"

"Yes?" his groggy voice said.

"After this we cook apart. That man *planned* to sponge

on us. I won't put up with it. He'll take advantage of any-body any way he can."

"Now, Libby—"

"Now your foot! Did we come a third of the way today?"

"No," Alister admitted. "Not by quite a lot."

"So will we make it to The Cascades in the three days we planned on?"

"If—"

"If, my maiden aunt! Our food won't last much longer than that, the way it disappeared tonight! And I'm not starving my family for the pure pleasure of hearing Mose Biggers belch!"

Alister found her hand under the blankets, gripped it tight. "We can't be uncivilized, Libby, even with people like that."

He wouldn't budge, so all she could do was hope that the wind died down, and it did not. The only difference she saw in the next two days was that each was more dis-couraging than the one before. On the first of these they awakened to find that, in the night, sleet had replaced the rain, with icicles hanging from the wagon sheets and waves washing over the deck of the raft. They could see that in the heights where Win was, new snow had fallen as well. They had inched downstream only a few miles, that icy morning, when a sudden crosswind tilted the raft, warning them of the danger of capsizing. So they put back ashore to wait again for the wind to die. It didn't come any closer to dying than Libby expected it to although the sleet changed back to rain. And the third day brought them no farther than the island the Indians called Memaloose, for there on high platforms they left their dead.

This was the first landmark, in a monotony of beclouded cliffs and muggy beaches, that they were able to identify with certainty. Alister knew its distance from the Dalles. That night, lying in the tossing darkness, he stunned Libby. They were, he whispered, hardly halfway to the cattle crossing where by then Win would be waiting, if something hadn't held up the cattle drivers, too.

"Oh, Alister," Libby moaned. "We're all but out of food! What will we do?"

"Well, we only have to reach the cattle crossing. Then we can butcher a cow, and that'll see us to The Cascades and the store."

"And there Mose Biggers will stock up or we *will* camp apart. I'm warning you."

"They're to be pitied, Libby. Life's made them what they are."

"Sometimes," Libby wailed on his shoulder, "your tolerance makes me furious!"

She had already forgotten the free land for which they had started upon this dreadful journey. Now she drew in her horizon until it reached no farther than the vague spot downstream where they would see Win. Somewhere below Dog River, she knew, the stock trail came off the heights to follow at water level until pinching bluffs forced it to switch to the north bank. She knew a ferry operated at the crossing in season, but her fear was that, like the steamboat *Flint,* it would have gone out of business for the winter by this time. If that proved the case, and the operator had left the gorge, the raft would have to be unloaded and the cattle ferried over on it. It boggled the mind to think of all the things that could confront them, even if Win was all right and they obtained fresh beef.

That night was the worst yet, and the next day they didn't even try to move farther downstream. This was enough to sober even Mose Biggers, and the two families stayed in the wagon boxes, hardly seeing each other all day. On the day following the wind slacked off enough to let them travel a few miles. It was the same on the next day and the day after. But it was never enough, and on the fourth day below Memaloose they had only come to Dog River. There the country was more open due to valleys that ran back on either side of the river. The wind was proportionately fiercer, and that night snow fell at water level for the first time.

During the black turbulence of that night Libby learned the true meaning of despair. They were a week out of The Dalles and not even at the crossing they should have reached during the second day. Even the Biggerses had seen the need to stretch the food the past few days. Even so, there wasn't enough left for more than one or two skimpy meals. At the rate they had traveled, it would take another three days to reach the cattle crossing. Listening to the sounds outside, she had no hope of maintaining their speed, let alone of increasing it.

It seemed unaccountable that she could awaken in the first weak rays of dawn with a strange lightness of spirit. Alister had left the raft, and she lay relaxed for a moment before she understood what, in the late night, had let her go to sleep. The raft rode quietly on the gentle waves of the river. There was hardly a sound outside. She rose quickly and looked out to see a whitened world on which fat flakes of snow fell peacefully. This should have been frightening and wasn't, and then she knew why.

The wind was down. They could raft. Maybe, God willing, all the way to the crossing before night. Alister wanted an early start, and as she came off the raft she saw him and Toby down the beach gathering firewood. Sarah and Amy were at the fire, but Mose was nowhere in sight.

Hurrying over the gangplank to the beach and fire, Libby said, "Good morning, Missus Biggers—Amy. Isn't this a welcome change?" Sarah looked at her with such a long face that Libby's breath caught, and she said quickly, "Why—is something wrong?"

"It's my man," Sarah said in a thin, flat voice. "He's sick. Can't lift hisself out of his bed this morning."

"No!" Anger charged Libby's voice, not sympathy, for she was thinking solely of the fact that it took three strong males to man the raft—the sweep and poles and lines. "Oh, wouldn't he? Just *wouldn't* he?"

Sarah pulled up her thin shoulders and hauled back her head. "You and me ain't had it so comfortable, Miz Arlen," a flatter voice said. "And we ain't worked out in that cold all day and on lean vittles, lately."

"I know," Libby said, ashamed of herself. "I'm sorry. What's the matter—the grippe?"

"I reckon he's just played out, Miz Arlen. He ain't as strong as he looks."

Libby turned away and then shut her eyes. Alister already knew about this horrible development on the one day when they might have made good progress, maybe even have gotten out of their plight. It explained why he and Toby were gathering so much wood when she had been so sure they would be leaving the camp within the hour.

Soup from the night before had already heated over the fire. When Sarah got a granite bowl and reached for the ladle, Libby lost her contriteness and spoke sharply. "Only for Amy and my children. We grown-ups will have to go hungry till we get more food."

Sarah glanced up with eyes as flat as her voice. "My man's got to build his strength, Miz Arlen. I was only fixin' to take a little to him."

Libby pulled in a long breath and nodded assent.

Sarah carried the filled bowl down to the raft, taking Amy with her, and disappeared into the rear wagon bed. Alister and Toby came in to drop armloads of wood by the fire. Toby looked longingly at the soup, but Libby frowned at him, prepared to keep him from it with a club if she must. He made no effort to help himself, and in a moment he turned and went down to the raft.

She looked at Alister and said urgently, "Was he so important we can't go on without his help?"

"Yes, Libby. It's not that there's so much to do except at the sweep and when we make land or shove off. It's the rocks. Sometimes it's all the polers can do to veer off from them."

"I can pole and handle lines. Alister? *Please?*"

"I—" Alister broke off, his face grim and leaking worry from every pore. She knew he wanted to try it, but he shook his head. "No. For one thing you can't leave the children unwatched while we're out on the river. Besides, we have no way of knowing this isn't a lull that'll be over within the hour. But we'll move camp and make a better one."

"Alister? Food?"

"That's what I have in mind, Libby."

Chapter 3

Libby had never seen Alister move with such fury. It was that of pace and manner rather than of temper. Yet it seemed to her that he must feel something of her cold anger against the Biggers, sick man or not, for he bossed Toby and hurried him. The two of them found a natural shelter down the shore, formed of the ever-present rocks. They moved the raft and camp there, and Alister drove Toby and himself setting up the most protected camp they had yet had. The fly covered it, wagon sheets closed two sides, sheer rock the back and to the wind if it rose again, and with a big fire roaring out front.

They might be safe from the elements, but what would they eat? Trapped fish? She wondered if that was what he had in mind.

The snow still drifted down in soft fat flakes, but he had destroyed her confidence in its staying so calm. So when Alister sent Toby to bring in drift and yet more drift and pile it near the shelter, she approved. Alister himself was moving their bedding up into the shelter since sleeping on a tossing raft was so close to impossible for her. Sarah and Amy hadn't emerged from their wagon box. Libby didn't know why Sarah had so stoutly refused to let Mose be moved into the shelter, also, when Alister suggested it. But she was glad that Sarah had.

When Alister had brought up the last of the bedding, he took her out of earshot of the children and spoke swiftly and decisively. "I'm going to make my way down the shore to the cattle crossing. I'll bring back meat and Matt Cowan to help us get the raft down that far as soon as we can."

"No!" Libby cried, understanding finally and appalled. She stared west toward the vaulting headland not far below them that seemed to drop into the water itself. "You'll never make it there and get back! Don't leave us here with—with them. I couldn't bear it!"

His hands dropped on her shoulders and shook them. "Hold onto yourself, Libby. It'll be rough going, but sooner or later I'll find where the cattle trail comes out of the mountains. Then all I have to do is follow that. I can't say how far the crossing is from there, but I'd guess it at ten or twelve miles. So I ought to be back tomorrow. You've food enough till then, and plenty of wood. Toby's a rough and surly boy, but he's still able-bodied, and you'll have him to help."

She thought of how afraid she was of Toby and cried, "Take us with you!"

"Impossible."

"If we can't make it, neither can you!"

"Hush."

"Send Toby! Except for them—!"

"If he got himself there safely, would you really rely on him to come back into this misery just to help us?"

The wildness went out of Libby, and she said weakly, "So you do understand."

"Yes. We could have had better luck in our traveling companions. But they need our help worse than ever now, and for a while it's up to you, Libby. You'll be the only strong one here."

She nodded, fortified by his faith in her, and he sealed his mouth to hers. Then he released her, stepped around the rocks and was gone. She couldn't watch this, anymore than she had been able to watch Win disappear into the dismal distance, back there.

She sat in the shelter with her children, who seemed to have left their tongues back at The Dalles. The fire filled the shelter with warmth, and the snow fell gently, and they sat where they couldn't see the raft floating on the quiet river. She tried to figure out the date, recalling day after day and camp after camp, and decided that it was the tenth of November. With only twenty days left in which to reach the Willamette, find their donation claim and file on it in the village that had assumed the name of Oregon City. Yet land wasn't as important as life, and that was the problem now. Life for her children and, God willing, for Alister and herself.

One by one the youngsters fell asleep in the snug warmth of which for so long they had had so little. Libby didn't know how long it had been since she had really slept for more than catnaps, yet she remained wakeful. But she grew sufficiently indifferent to her surroundings that Toby's appearance between her and the fire startled her and sent her heart racing.

Toby settled on his heels at the entrance of the shelter and looked at her more boldly than he ever had before. "Wal, you got it real cozy here, Miz Arlen," he drawled.

"I'd hardly call it that," Libby said frigidly. "How's your father?"

Toby grinned, shrugged his angular shoulders and said, "He'll live."

His unconcern hinted that he was used to such sick spells, and she frowned. "Has this happened before?" she asked.

"It shore has."

Suspicious without fully understanding why, Libby said, "Did my husband tell you what he was going to do?"

Toby nodded his shabby head. "Hope he makes it. I shore could use a meal."

"Did your father know?"

He glanced at her warily and shook his head. "Only what your man said yeste'day, when it was blowin' so mean. That we might have to tie up while somebody went down to the crossing for meat." He didn't let her reply to that, grinning at her slyly and adding, "You know it, Miz Arlen? You're a right purty woman."

Her back stiffened. "I can do without your opinion on that."

"No offense intended. It's just you don't see many purty

ones out here. Hope I find me one. Pa wants me to marry up quick so I can claim a six-forty next to his'n."

"Find and marry a girl in the next twenty days?" Libby gasped.

"It's done, Miz Arlen. They tell me strangers get married just so they can latch onto more land. Some fellers even take on a twelve-year-old girl, I heard."

"And I suppose you would."

"When they're big enough they're old enough to suit me. I just hope she's purty."

Toby rose then and drifted off along the beach, walking through the falling snow. Libby sat confronted by a crushing conviction that Mose Biggers' playing out was altogether too timely to be real. Yet it didn't hold up, for the day had dawned with a promise of their rafting to the crossing before dark, and the weather remained that way. She had to admit that her feeling came from her growing dislike of the man and her readiness to believe him capable of making sure he wasn't the one who had to undertake the grueling, dangerous trip to the crossing for meat.

The long afternoon ended with it proven that, had Mose Biggers held up, they could have rafted safely and at their best speed yet all day. Libby waited until the light began to weaken, then opened the kitchen box. Almost as if she had heard the hinges squeak, Sarah emerged from their wagon bed, bringing Amy with her as usual. Libby couldn't bring herself to ask about Mose, and Sarah made no report on him.

Neither she nor Sarah had eaten all day, and between them they had food enough for only one more kettle of conglomerate gruel that would have to be stretched among the children until Alister got back from below. They didn't speak of this and, together, prepared it. Amy sat beside Letty, who was the same age, and while the two girls rarely talked they seemed to draw comfort from each other's company. Yet there was a curious troubledness in Amy's face now.

When the gruel was ready, Sarah set out bowls for the children and the one extra. There was a gleam in her eye that reminded Libby again that the woman was as hungry as she was herself. She had all she could do to hold her tongue while Sarah ladled gruel for the weakling on the raft.

"Come along, Amy," Sarah said then. "We'll coax Pa to eat a mite, then you can come back for your'n."

Amy mumbled, "I want to stay here."

Sarah's voice sharpened, and she said sternly, "You come along, you hear?"

Libby had never before interfered with parental authority, but the misery in Amy's pinched, chapped face touched her heart. "Let her stay and eat with my children," she said quietly. "It's so much warmer here."

Sarah frowned at her and her mouth worked wordlessly. Then she shrugged and went down toward the raft with the bowl of gruel. Libby filled the children's bowls and passed them out. But when she came to Amy, the girl looked down at her grubby hands and stubbornly shook her head.

"Thank you kindly, but I ain't hungry."

"Oh, Amy," Libby said despairingly. "Don't you get sick on us, too."

Amy made a choking swallow, and then the awful words burst forth.

"Pa ain't sick."

Libby shut her eyes, for she had never really dissuaded herself of that suspicion. She said quietly, for it wasn't Amy's fault, "And he's been eating, along with you youngsters."

"No." Amy's little jaw stuck out angrily. "Ma and Toby et what she took down this mornin'. An' they're gonna eat it now."

"Your father hasn't eaten?" Libby gasped.

"He don't know anything about it. He's got a jug he bought up the river, and he ain't done nothin' but swill on it since last night. Now he's out senseless."

Libby felt an insane impulse to laugh. For this Alister was, at that very moment, risking his life. She remembered the fury of the previous night before the storm finally died down. Mose had expected to be storm-bound here, maybe to be the one forced to make the dangerous journey downriver for food, and he had escaped into his booze. The calm morning and day had found him too drunk to know that the day could have brought escape for them all.

After a long moment, Libby said, "You're a good girl, Amy. But I want you to have this soup. Please take it."

"I just ain't hungry. *You* eat it, Miz Arlen. You ain't et since yesterday."

Of them all, Libby thought bitterly, she and Alister who so had needed it before starting his journey. She knew now why Sarah had feared to leave Amy here. And she saw that she dared not confront them with it, for the child would suffer for it then or later.

She said gently, "I can't eat it, Amy, for the same reason you can't. I respect your feelings." She poured the gruel back in the pot. "And I won't let on that you told me."

"I don't care," Amy said defiantly. "I had to tell you so you'd eat. Please, Miz Arlen."

Libby wouldn't have believed an hour earlier that she could feel admiration for a Biggers. Her father lying drunk, her mother and brother cheating cynically—it had driven this small child to what must have been a painful act of disloyalty, a breach of discipline sure, as far as she had known, to bring punishment.

She couldn't render that for naught, and Libby said gently, "Will you share a bowl with me, Amy?"

"Well—if it's the only way you'll eat."

Libby got two bowls and ladled each half full. Her own children, not comprehending the depravity betrayed here, had finished their gruel. They watched Amy belie her lack of hunger, and Libby knew their own hunger was far from satisfied. She hardly tasted the hot liquid she swallowed herself because of the nausea in her stomach.

Sarah soon returned with an empty bowl. She had had at least half a bowl of gruel, herself, yet her eyes went greedily to the kettle that would be strained to feed even the children through the next day. She looked at Amy uneasily, then seemed to decide that the cat hadn't been let out of the bag.

But she wasn't running any more risks and said, "If you've et, Amy, come on."

"Let her sleep in the shelter tonight," Libby said quickly. "It'll be miserable on that raft."

Sarah's lips clamped together. She felt guilty and so was quick to resort to anger. "I reckon she can sleep where her folks do, Miz Arlen," she said. "If you don't mind."

"Very well."

Libby watched them go down to the raft and disappear. By then night had all but closed in on their chip of land under the mountain and beside the river. She watched the final coming of darkness, hating it because it was sure to have caught Alister short of his destination. The children grew drowsy and drifted off to sleep. Libby covered them carefully, then went out to put fresh wood on the fire, grateful to Alister for making Toby gather so much of it.

The storm came up again two hours later to surpass the one before. The new wind whipped the snow and shook the shelter until it threatened to go flying away, the fire and themselves with it. Almost as nerve-racking was the sound of it, a medley of roars and shrieks, with undertones of groaning forests somewhere far above and of booming waves that splattered the rocks of the beach.

Yet all through that sleepless night her mind was only indirectly on that spot and mainly on one she could only picture vaguely but horribly in an ever-worsening series flitting through her mind. A cliff at whose base Alister lay broken and helpless from a fall. A forest in which he wandered blindly in the cruel night. A slough into which he had blundered freezing and sucking him down. Even the ferry where he could have found Win sick from the terrible exposure of the mountains.

The next day was hardly better. While a sooty light leaked into the gorge, the snow kept falling. The killing wind kept blowing, and Alister wasn't able to keep his promise to return that day to his stranded family. But there was something on which Libby could fix her mind and turn her fear into loathing—the Biggerses except for Amy. Mose lay drunk on the raft all day. But Sarah and Toby emerged as usual in the morning, prepared to pull their sneaky trick again. Libby told them in no uncertain terms that there would be no gruel even for a sick man.

Only a miracle could bring Alister back that day, and even the children would be reduced to half-portions in order to stretch the contents of the kettle a day longer.

Toby's sly eyes went instantly sullen. Libby flung him a look of disdain, then looked again into Sarah's shifting eyes. Neither could stand against her, and they turned and went shuffling down to the raft. Amy hadn't put in an appearance and didn't all that miserable day.

The second night of her loneliness Libby found not quite so bad. The snow stopped falling. While still brisk and cold, the wind was down enough to be less alarming. She began to hope, for she could understand Alister's delay in returning in such a storm. If he got back with meat, she knew now that they could endure the cold and fatigue yet to be undergone before they got out of the gorge. She even managed to sleep, and while she slept it wasn't Alister who returned in her dreams. For no accountable reason, Matt Cowan appeared, huge and kindly and dependable. He carried big slabs of meat on his shoulders, and he told them not to be afraid for he would always take care of them.

Libby awoke instantly, her heart beating against her lungs. Then her ears picked up what might have been the cause of her dreaming. Although the other children seemed asleep, John was awake. He had been crying quietly, although he hushed when she stirred. None of the youngsters had eaten since morning, and then so little. She reached and put her hand on his brow and murmured reassuringly.

Her night-born hope began to leak away in the dawn. She freshened the fire, heated the pitiful last of the gruel and fed the children in the growing light, with a wretched half-bowl of it remaining in the kettle for Amy. The chores made her aware of an alarming weakness within herself which she refused to identify as hunger. Pouring the last of their food into a bowl, she went down to the raft, determined to see that it was Amy who ate it. When she came to the rear of the Biggers wagon box, she lifted the canvas flaps without warning.

They reminded her of grubs discovered from lifting a

rock, the way they were curled and packed together. Beyond the other three Mose was stretched flat, his upper body under the wagon seat, the rest of him taking up more than his share of the room. The jug was by his head, he was snoring loudly, and the smell that spilled out at her was that of sour liquor, his excrement and all their unwashed bodies.

She wanted to flee, but the jug that she had now seen with her own eyes let her speak without involving Amy.

"I must have misunderstood when you said he was sick, Sarah Biggers. Surely you must have said sickening."

"Now, there ain't no call," Sarah said in a slack-mouthed whine, "for you to be abusive. He is sick. He only took a little whiskey to ease his misery."

Ignoring her, Libby said, "I brought you some gruel, Amy, but this is no place to eat it. Come to the fire."

Amy's mouth worked silently. "I don't want it."

"Mebbe she'll want it after a while, Miz Arlen," Toby said. "Whyn't you leave it?"

"Come and get warm, anyway, Amy," Libby coaxed. "Letty'd like to see you."

"Thank you kindly, ma'am," Amy said with effort. "I reckon I better stay where I belong."

Chapter 4

Libby's first glimpse of Alister, when he came back to them, was of him staggering through the dusk under the weight of whatever he carried, and he came back without Matt Cowan. She had walked down the shore, leaving the younger children in Letty's charge. She hadn't gone far when her faintness told her she was wasting her strength, and she had been about to turn back when she saw him come out of the rocks and brush farther down. Even at the distance she could tell he was reeling, and she found herself running toward him, not in gladness but in renewed concern.

When he saw and knew it was she, he made an effort to steady himself but he still walked like a man driven unmercifully. It twisted her heart, and as she went running to him through the deep snow, her own weakness somehow changed into strength. His face was gaunt and bewhiskered and he had burning hollows for eyes, and seeing this nearly tore a cry from her throat. He put down his burden, and his arms reached out, and she fled into them, at last crying out.

"Are you all right?"

He nodded. "Are you and the children?"

"And Win?" she said nodding her own head. "Have you seen him?"

"He's at the crossing and well." Alister had to stop for

31

breath that rushed over cracked, bleeding lips. "I brought meat. About fifty pounds. We killed the heifer."

"Cowan?"

"I thought it best to leave him with the boys." Alister sucked in more air. "The ferryman's gone. We'll have to raft the cattle over. I didn't like the idea of leaving the boys there alone."

"No. But the rafting? Biggers wasn't sick. He was drunk that morning, Alister. He's been drunk ever since."

Alister's face turned black as the sky. "Did he give you trouble?"

"No." She decided not to tell him about Toby's lustful eyes and approaches. Nor of the trickery by which Sarah had got food for herself and Toby at the expense of the children. Or of Amy's astonishing sensitivity in the midst of so much coarseness. Alister still hadn't caught his breath, and she said in sudden anxiety, "Are you sick?"

"Oh, no." He managed to laugh. "A little tuckered, though. It was rough going. Especially coming back with a load."

Also hungry, exhausted and frozen, Libby thought, while Mose Biggers lay sodden and his lout of a son loafed and tried to be a lady killer. Then Alister bent to lift the sacked meat to his shoulder again, but she said, "No. You rest here, and I'll go get Toby to carry it."

His face darkened again. "We don't need them, Libby."

"No," Libby agreed. "But you do need me, and I'm going to help you, so hush now and let me."

Shared, the load was less of a burden, and they carried it between them to the camp. Because of the rocks the children didn't see them until they were nearly to the shelter. It was Letty who stood up, stared, let out a shriek and came running. The others were right behind her, arms flailing, legs pounding, even tiny Pip. They were half-starved, yet Libby knew it was the sight of their father that so enlivened them. Alister laughed, and they dropped the sack, then he tried to scoop them all into his arms at once.

Inevitably, the noise drew Toby outside on the raft. He stared toward them, then came walking up briskly, a hang-dog grin on his sharp features. He looked greedily at the sack and said, "Wal, I see you brung meat, Mister Arlen."

Rising unsteadily to his feet, Alister looked at Toby for a long moment. He had finally caught his breath, and he said coldly and evenly, "You people will eat, Toby, when you've brought your father out of there sober enough to help with the rafting. You'll eat only as long as he stays sober and pulls his weight. If he's too drunk to hear that, tell your mother and that I damned well mean it."

Toby looked at the ground, shuffled his feet and grew sullen. Then his gaze shuttled to the sack of meat, and he turned and went shambling down to the raft. Watching, Libby saw him stop on deck and dip a pail of water from the river. It was icy cold, and she knew where it would land, and the thought pleased her. Then she turned hurriedly to feed her starved family.

Alister had boned the meat so that every ounce he carried all those punishing miles would be food for them. Ordinarily she would have wished for something to go with it, but now the rich, red, lifegiving flesh seemed manna from heaven. She first thought to salt and broil chunks of it on sticks. Yet if it were boiled there would be nourishing broth, piping hot, which they all needed. So she curbed her impatience, prepared it, and got the kettle swinging again on the fire rod.

Then she heard Alister say quietly, "Look, Libby."

Following his eyes, she glanced down toward the river. Between them, Toby and Sarah were pulling and shoving Mose out on deck. He was bent at the middle but on his feet. When, on the deck, he fell to his knees, Toby turned calmly, dipped more water and sloshed it over his head. It was a miserable sight, yet the hardness hadn't gone out of Libby's heart.

Mose wasn't completely sober but he had been soaked, scrubbed and dressed in decent clothes when Sarah and Toby dragged him finally to the fire. He could at least hold himself upright and walk with a reasonable steadiness. Libby knew he was too sick to eat but couldn't pity him a bit. The meat was cooked by then, and she was about to start serving it when she realized that Amy hadn't come up from the raft. She didn't ask about her, instead turning and going down to see for herself.

The child sat huddled in the exact spot she had occupied that morning. Standing at the tailgate, Libby held out her hand and said gently, "Amy, as a favor to me, come to the fire and eat with us. There's plenty for everybody now. *Please?*"

Only then did the ice break up in the child's pinched face. Her mouth trembled, and her voice was small. "Miz Arlen? Ma says it wasn't right for us to blame Pa for what he can't help. She says he tries to stay sober, but he can only go so long."

Libby saw how dreadfully Amy needed her forgiveness, which she couldn't grant but could counterfeit. "I know, Amy, and I'm sure she's right. Come on now. Won't you?"

Amy's mouth trembled again, then she said, "All right."

For the first time since leaving The Dalles Libby felt safe that night. The meat diet might grow monotonous, but it would see them to the store at The Cascades. There was no new snow, the wind was down, and the river ran quietly enough to suggest that they could raft the next day. Alister still had no idea how far they had yet to go, regardless of his trip along the wild, untraveled shore. He could only measure it in terms of time, saying, after they were in their bed, that he hadn't found the cattle trail until daylight came the day after he left. It had taken much of the day to reach the crossing, butcher the heifer and get ready to return. In view of his experience going down, he had been afraid to start back at night under a heavy pack and without rest. He said nothing of the storm, the cold, hunger, the soul-draining weariness. He needed to say nothing. Having experienced that more moderately, herself, she knew what it was like.

It was nearly morning when she awakened to realize that he was restless. She reached out and touched him and said in a sharp whisper, "Alister! You're feverish!"

"No." He had been awake. "Just a little too tired to sleep well, I guess."

She said no more because she had to believe him. But

the hand she left on his breast told her he was hot—too dry and fever-hot to be merely tired.

He seemed all right in the morning, and Mose Biggers was sober, humble and hungry. Having failed so miserably, Mose now seemed bent on outdoing the other two men while the shelter was taken down, the camp packed and carried onto the raft. Libby felt only a cold indifference toward him. Because of what Amy had said, she tried to forget Sarah's trickery, too. In view of Toby's age, Sarah must have been married to Mose for some twenty years. She would have to use craft and low cunning to live, herself.

That day took them to the ferry, a bleak, bewintered spot where the south shore was broken by a shell-rock mountain, with the north bank flattened out. Win looked better than Libby had expected to find him in spite of Alister's assurances, and he was justly proud of himself for having helped bring the cattle over the wild, storm-battered mountains. And Matt Cowan—she simply looked up into his smiling eyes and experienced a strange lift of heart. She knew he wouldn't stay with them long—nor would Win—for once the cattle had been crossed over on the raft they would have to be trailed again. Yet she felt safer because of the strength in the gentle giant who was so unselfishly helping them.

It took all the next day to unload the raft and move the cattle over to the north shore. This was a perilous undertaking, for while the raft could be poled in the shallows, it could only drift on the main current and wait for the sweep to steer it in to land. The result was that it made land over a mile downstream from where it started, the handful of cattle held on by only a rope fence and threatening to capsize the lurching raft. And then, unloaded, the raft had to be poled upstream on the far side far enough to be steered back across on the current.

That night the wind came up again, for they were in a narrows that increased its force, and it brought instead of snow a hammering rain. Win, Matt and Dob Biggers had been left on the far shore, so that Libby's heartstrings were stretched painfully again, and the next day she conceived a new fear. The day took them hardly a third of the way to The Cascades, and the rain, while keeping them drenched, was warm enough that she was afraid the meat would spoil. They had picked up more of the heifer's flesh at the crossing, and at that night's camp she cooked as much of it as she could pack away in crocks. She hoped Matt Cowan would recognize the danger of the fresh meat he had taken with him becoming tainted. He had no way to preserve and carry it, and visions of them becoming stricken with ptomaine poisoning, over there, haunted her mind.

On the third day below the crossing they came to the dreamed-of Cascades. Instead of finding it an occasion for thanksgiving, the place only filled Libby with renewed despair. Alister seemed to have recovered from his over-taxing trip down the river. The cooked meat had lasted them, with enough left to get them past the rapids and onto the river again on the last lap. But, floating on the river, she had figured out that it was by then the eighteenth day of November. So there were only twelve days left in which to reach the valley and find and file on their full-mile square of free land. And the problem confronting them at The Cascades was dismaying.

Win, Matt and Dob were there, unpoisoned, with the cattle, and Matt had had time to look the situation over. That night in their camp below the store he described it, his heavy voice leveling out both pessimism and optimism. At that point, he said, the river narrowed down, constricted for several miles by rearing heights that once had been a single mountain sawed in two by the river. There were three series of rapids, Matt said, on just below their camp, another two down toward and at the bottom of this long stricture.

The water all the way was so fiercely swift that the wagons would have to be unloaded, set up on their wheels and pulled by the oxen over a very bad road running over the north point, a distance of about six miles. The raft itself would have to be floated down over the rapids, held captive at the end of ropes by men making their way along a very rough bank. Even without the rain it would be a difficult job. Yet thousands had done it before them, although in better weather and with plenty of others around to help.

Mose Biggers had listened big-eyed, and for the first time all the way he seemed to grasp realistically what they were up against. "Dag nab it, we're cuttin' her close," he muttered. "We can't afford to get hung up again or we'll miss out on the donation land."

"We could have gained a day or so," Alister said dryly, "if we'd had a full crew for the raft."

"A man's what he is." Mose's eyes flashed. "And don't you hide me about that."

Libby wondered at his sudden independence, now that food could be had easily and they were so close to the last stretch. But she shut it from her mind for she had lived with trouble too long to borrow it any longer, if she could help. She was curious as to why in a place so wildly isolated there was a store and sawmill. And about the little steamboat now cold, deserted and moored near the store. And the wooden tracks that ran down along the bank to disappear around the point below their camp. She asked Matt if he knew about this, and he did.

"It's the doings of the Bradford brothers," he explained. "I talked to one today at the store. They trade with the Indians. There's lots of 'em along here. In summer there's the emigrants coming down. There's traffic the other direction, too, military stores for Fort Dalles and the other forts on inland. Except for the Indians, it's all summer business, and that's why it looks so dead right now."

"Who owns the steamboat?" Alister asked.

"The Bradfords. It's called the *Flint* for a San Francisco man who's backing them. Man named Hendworth built the portage railroad to get around that haul we've got to make over the hill."

"Railroad?" Libby gasped.

Matt grinned at her. "That's what it is, ma'am. Wood rails and a car they pull along with a mule. It only runs down around this point here, Bradford told me. About a mile and a half. They can bring wagons up that far from below and haul on down past the other rapids to the lower river boats."

"Then why can't we go that way?" she asked.

"Like the steamboat, it's gone out of business for the year. Nobody here now but the man at the store and us and the Indians scattered about. The Indians are friendly. They've sort of been civilized by the old Hudson's Bay post that was down the river till the Americans took over the country."

Matt and Alister began to lay plans, with Mose Biggers offering nothing for all the rush he was in now. The other two men decided that the wagons would go over the hill together. The families would go with them, Mose and Toby handling the oxen, Dob and Win driving the loose cattle. Matt and Alister would take the unloaded raft down over the rapids, hoping to be there ahead of the others. If they were, they would have a shelter and fire waiting. The next morning the cattle could leave early on what Bradford had said was an easy, water-level trail to Fort Vancouver. The raft would be reloaded and launched on what should be smooth sailing to their final goal.

While the wagons were being set up and loaded the next morning, Libby went to the small store standing at the mouth of the creek that powered the sawmill. The Bradford on hand proved to be a bearded, courteous man of refined speech and manner. He was openly dubious about their trying to pull over the hill in that kind of weather, but he understood the urgency that drove them. She bought flour and coffee, beans and bacon, potatoes and dried onions, all sparingly, for their money was so close to gone. Before she had left the store, Sarah came in. It was a good thing she did for, had the Biggerses failed to provision, Libby was resolved to let them fend for themselves from there on. She didn't learn what Sarah intended to buy, for the woman waited until after she had left to order.

It was around eight in the morning when the wagons started. Mose went first with the Biggers wagon, then Dob and Win threw the half-dozen loose cows and heifers on the trail behind it. Libby wasn't pleased to find Toby as-

signed to drive the Arlen oxen, but Mose would have
suited her no better. Their wagon brought up the rear,
with Toby walking beside the oxen and haranguing them
steadily, Libby and Letty riding on the wagon seat, the
smaller ones lying on the load behind. Only once did
Libby look back, and she saw that Alister and Matt had
already started down along the bank, coaxing along the
floating and now-emptied raft. And then she settled herself to stare forward into a climbing, rainswept forest
that would surround them through most of that day.

The road followed up along the sawmill creek and was
from the start almost bottomless mud. The wagons that
had used it that summer and for several others had left
deep trenches that in the downpour had become small
creeks. The timber thickened, underskirted by dense, dripping brush. The oxen's hoofs sucked noisily as they were
pulled out of the mud, and Toby waded along clumsily,
plastered to the hips.

And then Letty's small voice said, "It's started to snow
again, Mamma."

Libby looked up from the mud ahead to see that this
was true. Wet flakes of snow, still in small quantity, were
mixed with the rain. "I don't think it'll make much difference," she said, although she wasn't so sure of that.

She wished Alister had come along to handle their wagon, with Toby helping Matt with the raft. She knew,
though, why it had been arranged this way. The lowering
of the raft over the rapids was by far the most difficult and
delicate undertaking. Matt and Alister hadn't wanted to
trust even a part of it to a Biggers.

Chapter 5

By midmorning the oxen had disclosed their weakness, for they had fared even worse than their owners all the way from the Missouri. The wagons were somewhere on the near side of the mountain by then. The road in many places was merely a notch cut into the side of a steep ravine, and the mud there was as deep as on the more level stretches. While the beasts threw themselves stubbornly against their yokes, it was all they could do now to keep going. Libby had climbed down from the wagon to lighten the load, helping Letty down with her. She had pinned up their skirts and now waded knee-deep in mud through what, as they climbed higher, had changed into snow without rain.

The Biggers wagon was usually out of sight around a bend, for Mose could manage a wagon better than Toby could. The loose cattle were even farther ahead, for they could pick their way and had traveled faster. So again Win was lost to her, as well as Alister, with the younger ones in her care and all of them in the dubious care of Toby. Toby was covered with mud from tip to toe by then, and sometimes he swore at the oxen. She didn't reprove him for this, for he had turned impatient and surly. She knew he could think of a thousand things he would rather be doing. He had nothing on her.

She had no idea of trouble ahead until she saw Mose come around the turn above, trudging through the snow-whitened mud toward them. Apprehension riffled through her, but she could gain no inkling of what was wrong until he had come down to where Toby had stopped the wagon. They exchanged a few low-voiced words, then Mose moved a step or so closer to her.

"Have to take Toby and your steers, Miz Arlen," he said, with something of the truculence he had shown Alister the night before. "My wagon's mired to the running gears up there. It'll take all four critter to haul her out."

"Oh, no," Libby protested.

"Well, you can't pull around me, that's certain. Only way I see is for us to double my outfit through, then come back and double you."

"How far ahead are you?"

"Just around that next turn."

"All right."

It was the delay and threat of worse going ahead that had dismayed her, for there had been many places, back on the trail to the Columbia, where the ox teams had had to double up. She watched them unyoke her oxen and drop the wagon tongue in the mud. They didn't say another word to her but simply went on up the awful road with the tired beasts. Libby looked up at the sky, filled with snow, and then off into the darkling timber. Much as she detested the two men she wanted to take the children and go ahead with them. Yet there were Indians somewhere near, and while they might not be hostile they could well be thieves. She would have to stay and watch their possessions.

Letty's small voice said, "How long's it going to be, Mamma? I'm cold."

"Not long, honey."

"Can we build a fire?"

"Where? And how could we get wood?" There were only steep banks above and below them. To go back to a more level place, where wood might be accessible, they would have to leave the wagon. "It'll only be a while. Be patient."

They scraped off as much mud as they could and got back into the wagon, out of the snow and wind. The younger ones still lay on the load in back, dry and so bundled they hadn't grown cold enough to complain. Libby wrapped a blanket around Letty, too, then sat on the wagon seat, staring glumly at the dropped wagon tongue. She wondered how Alister and Matt were faring with the raft.

With each minute dragging by on leaden feet it was impossible to keep track of the time. Yet she had enough sense of it to know when the Biggers men had had time to loosen the stuck wagon and come back. Yet the road above stayed empty. She began to feel a nameless apprehension, a vague but disturbing sense that more than she knew about was wrong.

She sat with this uneasiness until finally she had to do something. Making her voice as calm as she could, she said, "You children sit here nicely for a few minutes. I'm going to walk up there and see how they're coming. It can't be far. Just around the next turn, the man said."

They didn't like the idea of being left alone but didn't protest. Libby climbed down from the wagon. It was colder in the open air than it had been before. It seemed to her that the wagon had settled deeper into the mud even while standing still. The tracks left by the Biggers wagon ran with water. Elsewhere there was only snow-covered mud. She ploughed into it, not caring how splattered she got if only they could start moving again. Her foot hurt her, for she had a corn there and the cold had stirred it up.

She moved around the bend to see nothing on the stretch ahead. She hurried on. On the next turn, an inside one, she came to the place where the Biggers wagon had been bogged down but it was no longer there. Puzzled, she hurried around this turn, and then another outside one, and there still was nothing to be seen of their wagon.

They had gone on, but this didn't unnerve her completely. They might have decided to double their wagon over the summit before coming back to double hers. She went back down to the children and told them it would take longer than she had thought. She hadn't had time that morning to cook with the new provisions, so she crawled back to the kitchen box and got chunks of boiled meat out of a crock. They had grown tired of it but ate it obediently. She managed to choke down a few bites herself.

The deepening snow gave her a way to keep rough track of time. So much of it elapsed, she modified her theory, deciding that the Biggerses had tried to double to the summit before returning for her, only to get stuck again even with both spans of oxen. If so, and they couldn't get free, they would surely come down with all four steers and pull her wagon up to wherever theirs was. Then they could make camp, for all night if need be. But Alister and Matt had expected to reach the lower landing with the raft in midafternoon. If the wagons failed to appear by dark, they would strike up the road from that end. With their help the wagons could both get moving again, and all this would be over.

The children grew drowsy and napped. Libby kept watching the snow-whipped road ahead, on which nobody appeared, until they were awake again. By then she knew she had to make up her mind. Either they must strike off on foot or risk having to stay where they were all night. Afraid she was letting her urge to flee influence her, she waited a while longer. The snow was piling up, threatening to clog the road so badly that moving the wagon would be impossible even if they came. Then all at once she regretted that she had waited under such iron control so long.

Yet she kept her head and got matches out of the kitchen box in case they had to stop and build a fire. She squeezed the cold, greasy broth out of a few chunks of meat, wrapped them in cloth and put this in her coat pocket. Motion would help keep the other children warm, but she would have to carry Pip. So she wrapped a blanket around him. She told Letty to walk ahead with John and Margaret, and they started out up the mountain.

By the time they passed the place where the Biggers wagon had been stuck, snow had smoothed everything out but the swift little streams running in the wheel ruts. When, nearly worn out from carrying Pip and with her bad foot throbbing like a toothache, she took the little band over the summit, the light was fading from the whip-ping air. She refused to draw conclusions from the fact that the Biggers wagon had not been found below them and wasn't at the summit. All her thoughts were on the three small bodies that somehow kept floundering through the snow, mud and water ahead of her.

A little after dark Margaret fell flat in the mud and in-stead of trying to get up began to cry. Libby shifted Pip to her hip and with her freed arm lifted Margaret. She had no doubt that the older two wanted to cry, for she did, also. But by now Alister would begin to realize some-thing was wrong, and he and Matt would strike off up the road to meet them. She considered stopping to build a fire and wait for them. Yet she didn't *know* that they had got through with the raft on schedule. They might not make it to the lower landing at all that night. She went on until her aching foot became unbearable. Then she stopped the older children, put down the others and took off the shoe and stocking. The cold, muddy wetness felt good to the fevered foot. They went on again.

It was long after nightfall when they came out of the timber and the grade lessened and finally leveled off in the open. The snow fell less heavily at the lower level, but Libby could see no campfire anywhere ahead. Yet she could see well enough to follow the road, and they stumbled on. The road was curving, she noticed, bending them down toward the river, and still there was no fire anywhere at all. She didn't let herself puzzle about this, either. There was an answer to everything and she was afraid of it.

The first indication that they were near the lower land-ing came when she heard the sound of a complaining cow somewhere off to the right. It was no trick of the senses, for the children heard it also, turned their heads and seemed to perk up. It meant that Win had got here, at least, and the cattle had been turned loose on the wild pasture. Probably rocks or brush kept her from seeing their campfire. And probably—but why had no one come up the road to meet and help them?

And then they were at the river, and there had been nothing to keep the fire and camp screened so she couldn't see it. There simply was no fire, no camp, no people, no Biggers wagon. Yet it was the place, for the road reached it and stopped. She remembered the cow she had heard. Someone else's—perhaps an Indian's?

Letty said in strangled urgency, "Mamma, where *are* they?"

Libby fought sheer panic then. She waited a long moment, swallowing, then managed to say with reasonable calmness, "I don't know, honey. Maybe we missed a fork, and the camp's up or down the river from here. We won't hunt for it in the dark. We'll build a fire and get warm. Then maybe someone will see the light and come and get us."

"Why haven't they come, already?"

"Don't fret, honey. We'll have to wait and ask them when we see them."

There was plenty of drift, and she gathered it. She used splinters for kindling and, with feelingless hands, got a small fire started. Its blaze and light helped calm her, and the children crowded about. She added more wood, an expert with a bonfire now, having cooked over so many. She fed and watched it grow because it kept her eyes off this spot that seemed so like that of the dead. She didn't care about the Biggers family. Where were Alister and Win and Matt? Indians? No, they were said to be used to white people and friendly toward them.

She gave the children the meat from her pocket. They were exhausted, soaked to the skin, and splattered with mud to their hair. While they ate she drew her stocking over a swollen, muddy foot. It was no use. She couldn't get on the shoe she had carried. She piled more and more wood on the fire.

It was quite a while later she heard a shout from up the river, a male voice that still wasn't a man's. Libby sprang to her feet and started off through the now thin snowfall, still seeing no other fire yet knowing hers had finally been seen. It came to her, like icy fingers on her heart, that it could have been a call for help. She started to run pell-mell toward the sound then checked herself, knowing she couldn't leave the children there alone. She turned back and waited, and presently the night parted and produced Win.

He was as muddy as the other children but looked all right physically, yet his face was graven with fear and concern. He had been running and cried, "Mamma!" breathlessly, then gulped and said, "Mamma—!" again.

Calmness came from somewhere, and Libby pulled him to her. "What is it?"

"The—raft got away from them—papa got hurt—his leg—where are the wagons?"

Libby was glad he had his face pressed against her and couldn't see hers. She couldn't take it all in, so she asked the question longest in her mind, "Why, haven't you seen the Biggerses?"

Win shook his head. In a moment he had calmed down enough to tell her more coherently what had happened, and while she listened Libby fought to keep control of herself. He and Dob had got in with the cows in mid-afternoon, Win said, and turned them loose on the grass. They had been interested in the undertaking of bringing the raft down over the rapids. So instead of waiting there for the wagons they had taken the road that ran up the river shore from there and was used by the portage people. They had found his father and Matt at the middle rapids, about two miles upstream, where disaster had struck them not long before.

The rapids there were shattered by rocks and very swift. The men had barely started guiding the raft through them from the high bank when it hit a submerged rock and up-ended. The line Alister held had jerked so hard, so unexpectedly, that he had gone flying into the air to land in an unbroken fall on the rocks below. He would have gone on into the swirling waters and drowned if Matt hadn't leaped down to help him. The raft had gone banging down over the rocks below and broken up.

Matt had managed to get Alister back up on shore, unconscious, half-drowned, hurt so badly that moving him any farther without some kind of conveyance was out of the question. There was an Indian village not far away, Win said, but none of the Indians had wagons. So Matt

had built a fire and made a crude shelter to dry them out
and keep Alister warm, and not long afterward Win had
arrived with Dob. Matt had sent Dob back to the lower
landing to wait for the wagons and tell his father to unload and bring one of them up the portage road as soon
as they got in. That was the last they had seen of Dob.
Night had come, and finally Matt had sent Win down to
see why no wagon had come.

"And where are they?" Win asked again.

"Well, ours is on the other side of the mountain," Libby
said in a voice that sounded like a stranger's. "The
Biggerses must have strayed off the road somehow. With
all the snow, I couldn't see their tracks."

"Then," Win asked, "where's Dob?"

"I don't know." Libby shook her head bewilderedly.
"He didn't come up the other road to meet us, or I'd have
seen him." She had taken the avalanche of disasters more
calmly than she would have believed possible. Without the
raft they were all helpless, but that was nothing compared
to Alister and his poor broken body, hurt maybe beyond
recovery. Despair would do no good, she had to think
what to do for him and of nothing else. She added quietly,
"You stay here, Win. Get warm and take care of your
brothers and sisters. I've got to go up to Papa."

Letty wailed, "Take us with you!"

"Honey, it's another awful long walk. Besides, somebody's got to be here if the Biggerses get in and tell
them to come up with their wagon."

She turned hastily and left them, walking off into the
darkness, the weariness that had nearly dropped her, coming down the mountain, forgotten completely. The snow
was less deep down here, and the road hadn't been so
badly cut up by wagons. She walked swiftly, yet it seemed
a long while before she smelled smoke and saw pale specks
of light that she knew marked the Indian village. They
had dogs that barked, but none came out to harass her,
and she went past this. She was in under the mountain
then, nearly crowded into the river, but the road went on
and she followed.

Only a little later she saw the glow that made her

heart contract. She went faster, almost running. She saw a big figure move between her and the fire and she called. The figure came toward her.

She didn't understand at first why Matt stopped her before she had quite reached the fire and the still figure she saw there, covered by blankets he must have got from the Indian village. He loomed over her, and his heavy, gentle voice said, "Miz Arlen—Miz Arlen—" And then he dropped his big hands on her shoulders and looked down into her eyes. "You got to be brave, Miz Arlen. He's dead."

Chapter 6

Firelight danced on the side of the wagon, which Matt had that day brought down from the mountain. Morning had disclosed that the Arlen oxen, still yoked together, had been left with the three Arlen milk cows in the wild pasture. Day had also told Matt, who had been more discerning than she could be that morning, of the ugly drama in human frailty that had reached its climax at that spot. He talked about that now, in the evening. Libby knew this was to get her mind off what he had helped her to do that day—lay Alister to rest forever in this wilderness where his young life had ended.

Her children were sleeping in the wagon, too young to know what had happened to them. Libby sat by the fire, not wanting to go in there to lie down without Alister beside her. Matt had unrolled his bed under the wagon, but he remained at the fire, still trying to help where no one could help her.

There had been a wharf boat here, he said now. Bradford had told him about it at the Upper Cascades store, suggesting that they could use it for shelter if the weather proved mean down here. It had been empty, although in summer it was used as a landing by the steamboat that came up this lower reach of the river from the towns on the Willamette.

"I don't reckon Mose planned any of it ahead," Matt said. "He just kept seein' chances to advantage himself and grabbin' 'em. Itchin' to get to the valley, the free land, before the time runs out."

The way Matt reconstructed it, Mose had reached the lower landing in mid-afternoon, maybe intending, with his own wagon safely through, to go back with the oxen or send back for her wagon. But Dob had been waiting there to tell him the raft was lost and Alister hurt badly. To take time to build another raft, to wait there until an injured man was recovered enough to travel, had been more than Mose could abide. The wharf boat was half again as big as the raft and had a deckhouse. So, instead of taking the wagon up for Alister, Mose had loaded it, his oxen and milk cows and family aboard, and cast off.

"Would it have saved Alister's life," Libby asked, "if he'd come up with the wagon and got him?"

"To say would be to pass judgment on the man, ma'am. I ain't smart enough to say."

"Alister nearly killed himself to get food for them," Libby said fiercely. "As well as for us. I hope they drowned."

"Not likely. I reckon they only went down as far as they could get by dark and tied up."

"Small loss to the world if they had."

"Well, now," Matt said gently. "That Dob wasn't so bad. I sort of come to like him, crossing the mountains. Your Win took to him, too."

"Dob went with them, knowing we were all being abandoned to our fate."

"His daddy probably made him," Matt said. "Mose needed his help, too."

"You're a tolerant man, Matt," Libby said. "Like Alister was. But I'll hate them all to the day I die."

He glanced at her quickly, as though surprised that she could feel that one emotion when she had betrayed no other. She hadn't cried, even there at the middle rapids when he told her. She must have swayed, for suddenly she found herself with his arm across her shoulders, supporting her. Then the numbness, and a mind stopped like a clock. With Alister beyond danger of further pain and injury, Matt had taken him up in his arms and carried him all the way to the lower landing. In the morning he had convinced her that it was impossible to take Alister on with them, that he must remain here, and so they had consigned him to the earth.

Now the awful day was done, and finally she said with a gentleness that matched Matt's, "You ought to sleep. I'll just sit a while yet by the fire." When he shook his head, she thought he was afraid to leave her alone with her thoughts and added, "I'll be all right."

He looked at her intently, and she realized there were more problems facing her. He said, "Have you given thought yet to what you'll do?"

"Go on and take land," Libby said. "That's all I can do."

"But Miz Arlen. It can't be done."

"There's ten days left. I'll help build a raft. They say it's smooth sailing from here."

His eyes were pained. "That's not what I'm getting at, Miz Arlen. It's the law. I hate to have to tell you, on top of the other. But to take up land under the donation act, you've got to be an American citizen, eighteen or over—and male."

Libby's mouth dropped open. She had felt something finally, although only a jar, a shock. "Oh, no."

"I'm scared it's the truth."

"How'll I ever support my children?" she moaned. "What will I do?"

"I thought we'd best talk that over, ma'am. Do you have kin or friends back east?"

She shook her head numbly. "None I'd ask to take care of us. And how'd I get back there, if there was? Oh, no, Matt. You must be wrong."

"I wish I was, ma'am, but I'm scared I'm not. You talk like a woman with learnin'. Could you teach a school?"

"I don't have uncommon learning, Matt. Alister did, and between us we'd have taught our own children. But a school? They can only pay a pittance on the frontier, and how could I bring up five children that way? I've got to have land. Alister knew we'd need it even if he practiced law."

But land was out of the question, and Matt said doggedly, "Could you do sewin'?"

"Well enough. But what settler woman could or would hire a seamstress? Or a washwoman?" Her head began to ache, and she couldn't think about it any longer. Knowing he wouldn't go to bed with her still up, she got to her feet. "I'll say goodnight, now. But I want to say this. You're a fine man, and if I live another hundred years, I'll never stop being grateful. But you go on now and find your own land before it's too late. Just send a boat up for us from Fort Vancouver. We'll be all right till it gets here."

"No, ma'am. For one thing I'm not a married man, and the time limit don't affect me. A half section's all I could get today, and I can still get that next week, next month, next year."

"You're not a married man." Libby lifted her hand to her mouth and shook her head. "Oh, no. What's wrong with me?"

He rose and stood before her, watching her eyes. "I thought of that, too, ma'am," he said quietly. "As a last resort."

"No. It's impossible. It's shocking. Goodnight."

The next day Matt went back to the timber and began to cut logs for a new raft, Win helping him. Libby wanted to help, too, but Matt told her to stay at the camp and mind the younger children and not to be afraid. He had a little money, probably more than she had for he hadn't had a married man's expenses in the East. There was still the store at the upper rapids. Even if they found themselves stranded at The Cascades for the winter, they could make out well enough.

This did comfort Libby, and it comforted the children for they liked Matt and felt as safe with him as they had with their father. So she kept her mind off the fresh grave nearby, and for the first time really looked at this place where everything had come to such a sudden and crushing end. Two big islands stood off from the lower landing. And here and for some distance downstream the hills lay well back from the river, the slopes gentle and open, the background formations not high. The place was actually beautiful, even with winter on it, and this also was a comfort for Alister must stay here until the end of time.

That night, after the children had been put to bed, she mentioned this to Matt, and he agreed. "It's good land, too," he said. "A man could do worse than stakin' his claim right here. There's enough good ground for quite a few claims, too. But Bradford was tellin' me he thinks there'll be a town here, instead of a farm community. Or maybe both."

"A town?" Libby asked.

"Bradford's got high hopes for the inland, ma'am. It's got good land itself, some as fertile as the Willamette country. He thinks there'll be communities like The Dalles clean up the river and all the sidestreams. The Cascades, here, is the key to it. Everything's got to pass through."

Libby tried to picture the town that might grow here, thinking how wonderful it would be if there was one already. Then she could stay with Alister and bring up his children here and die here herself. "It could be. I wonder how soon it'll come?"

"The Willamette's already pretty full. Bradford says the next rush'll be to the interior, as soon as the Indians up there have been taught to behave. The army figures it's got to do that sooner or later, and that's why it's built all them forts."

"Matt? Why don't you take your land here? In time, maybe, I could buy part of it from you."

"Well, if I had to beat the deadline, I'd do that rather than gamble on finding somethin' better down below."

She sighed. "It could have solved that problem for Alister and me, too."

He nodded his head. "A six-forty would take in all this by the river and run back into the timber, too. A man could farm and make extra money cuttin' wood for the steamboats. A woman could sell milk and butter, eggs and garden truck to the travelers."

Knowing she was thinking only of the children and herself, Libby pressed with the question he hadn't answered. "Why don't you take a half-section here, anyway. Then when you get your patent you could sell me part of it. I'd find some way to pay for it."

"Well, there's where the law butts in again. A man can't take homestead land with the idea of selling it or even part after he's proved up. They had to put restrictions like that on it, or there'd be all kinds of trickery. But—" He hesitated, looked at her keenly, then spoke in a yet softer voice. "There's what you started to say last night, Miz Arlen. Maybe it's trickery, too, but you're entitled to land. You'd have had it except for your misfortune."

She met his eyes, was drawn again, but had to shake her head. "It came to me last night, but I couldn't do it. There's only one man I ever loved or ever will. Even if it wouldn't be a scandalous thing, him just in his grave, I couldn't."

"I'd never consider it anything but an arrangement to help you, Miz Arlen. I'd ask nothing and lose nothing, for I'd have my own half-section that way or the other way."

"It would be disgraceful," Libby said weakly. "Selfish of me. Unfair to you."

"But you want to do it?"

"Because of my children," she said. "I do."

"Then we don't need a raft to take down the wagon. All we need is somethin' to get you, me and the young ones to Oregon City. To—have it done and file and then come back."

"Oh, Matt."

He sprang to his feet and walked off into the night. She knew he was going up to the Indian village for they had boats, not large enough for a wagon but large enough for a few people. She looked into the wagon and saw that the children slept. Then she turned and went along the river to the grave.

The night was still, not cold, and she could see stars across the sky. She tried to pray, only to find that she couldn't. If God had let this happen, he would hardly bother to show her what to do. Then she looked down and said as she had on so many other troubled nights, "Alister? I won't be his wife. He isn't asking that of me. And I so want to own this land where you'll be and live and die on it and be buried here with you."

She was in the wagon though not asleep when Matt came back, and she knew he had arranged for a boat. Later she slept, spared the need to find more answers for at least a while. The next morning two Indians came down from the village in a dugout. The children, not understanding what great changes had been and would be made, went aboard without questions. Then Matt helped her in and got in himself, and they were on the way to the Willamette of which she had dreamed so long.

She never really made the trip, although she lent her physical presence to it. The Indians were good boatmen and took them as far as Fort Vancouver, once a fur post, now a military establishment with a village grown up around it. Another boat took them across the Columbia and up the Willamette to the town where falls broke the river. Matt found a minister of the gospel and it was done and he put up his new wife and family at the inn while he went alone to file the claim.

While they waited, Libby told the children that Matt had become their new father. That was all she said for the adult, intimate reservations were beyond their comprehension. Matt was gone quite a while, and when he returned he looked relieved and yet disturbed.

He said, "Well, it's done, Miz Arlen."

For the first time since leaving The Cascades Libby felt something. Again it was only a shock, a jolt of her deadened nerves. For in that one second she realized that the term of address he had used had been dissolved forever while they stood before the minister.

She managed a smile and said quietly, "No more Miz'es and ma'ams, Matt. I'm Libby. And you've filed on the land?"

"It's our'n." He told her about it. The territorial map was a good one, he said. He had been able to identify everything well enough to lay out the claim by the well-defined landmarks. It covered the part she so wanted

Chapter 7

Standing off the Dalles City waterfront in the flatboat by which he had brought up cordwood to sell, Matt remembered a blustering November morning four years past. Again he saw the Arlen and Biggers families, and himself, preparing to start on the last lap of their journey to the Willamette Valley. His mind pictured the women and children huddled at the fire of their last camp. It saw the men putting the final touches on the raft. He remembered his own deep uneasiness when he, Win and Dob started onto the mountains with the beat-out cattle.

Now an enlarged military fort stood on the slope up Mill Creek, back from the river. The old buildings of the church missions were vacant and falling apart. The Indian village had been pushed off to Celilo Falls, at the head of the rapids that broke up the river upstream. Where there had been only the tiny store and a handful of cabins, there now stood a humming town of five hundred people. There still was a little order to the residential district, but the business section ran neatly along the river bank, and the street was called Front.

False-fronted buildings lined the avenue eastward from Mill Creek, housing the variety of establishments needed by a town that had become the jump-off for the interior and the center of a local cattle industry. The busiest were a large general mercantile store and several smaller stores. Due to the through traffic, there were three hotels, a boardinghouse and several restaurants. There was a livery barn adjoining a saddler's, a bakery and an apothecary's shop. Spaced between was a total of twenty-seven saloons.

Preparing to start the return trip to The Cascades, Matt thought of Alister Arlen and the irony of their haste to leave this spot only to rush into misfortune and disaster. There had been abundant land available here, and already there was a town in need of a man of the law. A year ago, with Dalles City its seat, Wasco County had been created to include all the country east of the mountains and south of the river. . . .

Matt came out of his thoughts to see that Win, who had helped him that summer, had cast off the lines and was looking up at the wheelhouse where Matt stood in the stern of the barge. Maybe it was Win who had made him think of Alister, for at fifteen the boy was the spit and image of his father. Matt tipped his head in a nod, and Win went to the bow capstan and lifted the anchor. He was brown as an Indian, light-moving and quick. He hurried back past the wheelhouse and stepped into the skiff astern. Rowing, he towed the flatboat out into the stream. Matt grinned at him, then glanced on to where a September sun bathed the north bank hills. That side of the river had been cut off from Oregon to form Washington Territory a couple of years before. So many changes and yet so much, to Matt, that had not and would never change, like the hardness in Libby's heart that would never let him get near her.

The current caught the hull, and while Matt swung the craft on into the channel, Win came back aboard and climbed to the wheelhouse. His voice, changed now to a baritone, was eager. "Want me to take it, Matt?"

"Don't reckon I've worn myself out, already," Matt teased.

Win looked so disappointed that Matt laughed and turned the wheel over to him. Leaning against a window ledge, he got out his pipe and tobacco. They had come up two days before and spent the previous day unloading the wood they had brought and sold to a local woodyard. With the early start, and barring trouble, they would be home by late afternoon, and he knew Win wasn't looking forward to the return. If his mother would permit it, he would spend all his time on the river if he could. Or at Matt's wood ranch or one of his own yards that supplied fuel for the steamboats at The Cascades.

Win handled the wheel well, and they were soon sliding down the quiet reach of water to Crate's Point. Matt lighted his pipe and looked out at the empty deck ahead. It was much lower than the wheelhouse to give the pilot good vision when the deck was loaded with wood. Up forward rose a tall mast to which top- and main-sails had been yarded on the trip up to draw power from the westerly wind. The sails were furled now, and the topsail had been rigged across the bow. Weighted with rocks and submerged, this substituted for the wind and drew pulling power from the river current itself.

They had rounded the point and nosed into the wind when the *Mary* sounded her whistle upstream and behind, downbound on one of her triweekly runs to The Cascades. Looking back over his shoulder, Win grinned. He loved the flatboat Matt had put into service at the start of that summer. But it couldn't hold a candle, in his eyes, to the *Mary* or *Wasco* or *Fashion* or *Belle,* all of which now called regularly at The Cascades.

"Don't try to outrun her," Matt said jokingly. "Just get over and let her past."

Win laughed, for the *Mary's* side-wheels would soon show them her heels. He veered toward the north shore, then said wistfully, "Doggone it, Matt. Can't you talk Mamma into letting me keep on working for you?"

Matt's brow darkened. This was the last wood run they would make upriver until the coming spring. "I'm not even going to try," he said. "You know why as well as I do."

Win wrinkled his nose and said, "Yeah. School."

"School," Matt agreed. "And what's wrong with that?"

"Nothing, I guess." Matt didn't like the sullen eyes the lad turned back on the river. After long minutes, and with the *Mary* overtaking them swiftly, Win added, "Dob's going on the river next summer. Cap Baughman's promised to sign him on."

It was Captain Baughman's boat passing them. Matt frowned toward it. "Dob's a mite older'n you. Anyhow, your ma's not likely to be influenced by his example."

"Dob's all right," Win said stubbornly. "And so's Amy."

Privately, Matt agreed. Mose Biggers had proved himself as shiftless on his land as elsewhere and had spent most of his time at The Cascades, lying around full of booze. Toby was a little better, and the two of them managed to keep Libby's hatred of the family stirred up. But it ought not to include Dob and Amy. Matt had long since learned that Dob had told his father about Alister lying hurt up the river and in need of the wagon. Dob had been told to shut up and forced to take part in the desertion. It had done something to Dob he would never get over, and the same was true of Amy.

The *Mary* slipped on downstream, and the slower flatboat came to the mouth of the Klickitat. This river drained a big plateau running north into Washington Territory, and on beyond the mountains was the valley of the Yakima. Both regions were Indian country, and this made Matt think of something he had heard the night before in Vic Trevitt's saloon in Dalles City. Matt didn't know if it boded well or ill for the river settlements.

There had been Indian trouble in one place or another ever since he arrived in the country, starting with the Snakes along the emigrant trail and spreading to the Rogues in southern Oregon. Shock waves of this had not been long in appearing in the Columbia country, resulting in the strengthening of Fort Dalles and the dispatch of ten civil militia companies from west of the mountains into the interior. While an uneasy treaty with the inland Indians had been secured, it now turned out that some of the chiefs had signed only because of the military force gathered against them. The more fiery ones were reneging, for their best valleys were swiftly being occupied by white settlers. In addition, cattle grazers took in herds to crop off the grass. Gold strikes on the Fraser and upper Columbia brought in miners by the thousands, a loose-footed, irresponsible breed that was the worst resented. These crossed Indian country in strong companies, stealing, abusing and often raping the young women.

The Klickitats and Yakimas were the most warlike, although the Walla Wallas and Cayuses were in sympathy. All four bands were said to have held a secret council at the village of Kamiakin, the Yakimas' young chief. There it had been agreed that any white miners attempting to cross their country thereafter would be killed. The upshot was that Sub-Indian Agent Bolan, a good friend of the Yakimas, was caught alone in Yakima country by three young hotbloods and killed. As a result, Major Haller had left Fort Dalles with two companies of regulars to deliver a reprimand. The Yakimas jumped and shot up his command, which barely managed to escape back to the fort. The effect had been the opposite of pacification.

What Matt had heard in Dalles City was that later intelligence put the number of hostiles at a round thousand, a much larger force than the white people had supposed. They had long had guns, for this was old Hudson's Bay Company territory. From somewhere they had obtained a staggering store of ammunition. Now they had the heady impetus of having routed the soldiers they once had feared.

A special worry about this had stuck in Matt's mind. The Cascades owed its own growth to military traffic as much as to the influx of settlers and miners, and this was likely to grow greater still. Yet the Klickitats roamed country perilously close to the portage, and the Yakimas were only a skip and a jump farther off. So far The Cascades Indians had been passive and harmless, but it would be foolhardy to count on that holding true. White settlements had sprung up at all the rapids, with homesteaders venturing out as far as Beacon Rock below and Wind River above. More and more they had become contemptuous of the natives, crowding them out of desirable locations. The army had disclosed an awareness of this, and of The Cascades' strategic importance, by placing detachments of regulars at both the upper and lower landings. . . .

Matt turned his head, for another whistle had sounded

upstream. This signal came from the *Wasco,* which only a month before had been put in competition with the *Mary.* Captain Van Bergen commanded her, connecting with the *Fashion* below and using the Oregon shore to portage by pack train over a rough trail. The whistle pulled Win's head around with the same interest he had shown in the *Mary.* Matt shook his own head regretfully. Too bad the boy's mother had never taken a good look into his heart.

Noon found Matt at the wheel, with Win below in the cramped cabin making them a meal. They were approaching Dog River by then, with the White Salmon pouring into the Columbia from the Washington side. Not far below was the place where, on a storm-battered beach, Libby and her small fry had been left in the dubious company of the Biggers family. Matt thought of Alister's grueling walk to bring back beef, not knowing yet that the sick Mose was merely senseless with booze from his secret jug. That was where it had really started, everything that had changed Libby's life and Matt's own.

Below Wind Mountain the river grew wider only to narrow abruptly at The Cascades. The mountain abutment creating the rapids was all on the Washington side and, from the distance, seemed to stand squarely across the river itself. But, as Matt had long ago learned, the water escaped out of the southwest corner of this, hurtling and crashing through the upper rapids' fan-like rocks. In the opposite corner of the seeming bay was the upper settlement.

There at the Bradfords' wharf the *Mary* was putting ashore the freight she had brought down from Dalles City. At the same time she took aboard a much greater quantity of military stores and commercial shipments to Dalles City. The portage cars were there from below, and the transfer with the lower river packet would keep the steamer there through much of the following morning. On the opposite side, against an empty shore, the *Wasco* was going through the same procedure.

Upstream from the Bradford sawmill was Matt's woodyard, just beyond the tent camp of the thirty soldiers stationed there. The water there was slack, and Matt had put in his own dock so the steamers could put in handily for fuel. There at the end of the afternoon he and Win docked his own small river craft. Win's long face showed that he was even more aware than Matt that his fine summer had reached its end.

Walking from the wharf into a dusty, cluttered area of wood ricks, Matt said, "Well, boy, you best get on home. It's been a while since you saw your mother."

"Aren't you coming?" Win said in surprise.

"In a day or so," Matt said vaguely. He knew Win hadn't lost his boyish pleasure in riding the portage cars and added, "If you hustle over there, you can go down with the train, maybe."

Win nodded but still looked puzzled. None of Libby's children understood why he was so much away from home when there was no estrangement between him and their mother. Even yet Win was too young to understand how a man might prefer that to the painfulness of a life with Libby that had no real intimacy in it.

"Better get a wiggle on," Matt urged, "or you'll have a six-mile walk."

"Yeah. See you tomorrow, maybe?"

"Maybe."

"Then so long."

"So long."

Matt watched the lad hurry away to catch the portage cars before they started back to the lower landing for another load. Then he went deeper into the yard to where Gabe Hadley was loading wood on a wagon. Hadley's job was to keep enough wood ricked on the wharf to fill the wood racks of a steamboat, and both steamers would load fuel before they started back upriver. Matt talked with him for a while, then left the yard and walked along the shore toward the village. His pause had been only to make his parting with Win a little easier.

By the time he reached the store, the portage cars were slipping around the point below the town. To his surprise, Win wasn't on them but, instead, stood on the porch of the store. Matt saw why instantly. Two horses stood hipshot at the tie-rack. Their burlap saddlebags showed they had been ridden to the store for supplies. Their riders were on the porch, talking with Win.

They were Dob and Amy Biggers, and all three grew hushed when they saw Matt coming toward them. This bothered Matt, for while he did his best to be the kind of substitute father Libby wanted, there were ways in which he differed with her rules for her children. These youngsters knew she didn't like her offspring having truck with any member of the Biggers family.

Instead of showing disapproval, as they expected, Matt said, "Howdy, Dob. You, too, Amy. Girl, you get prettier every time I see you."

It was no lie, and maybe a fact known to Amy herself, but his voicing it took from her fresh young face the faint sullenness. At thirteen she was tall and slender. Her thick dark hair was neatly combed, although much of it lay on her shoulders. She granted him a shy smile, and he saw teeth white and even. Her dress was calico but hadn't been cut in the baglike looseness so favored by settler women.

She said, "Thank you kindly, Mister Cowan."

Although both had about reached the limits of their physical growth, Dob stood half a head taller than Win. He, too, looked uncertain and uncomfortable.

"I'm going to ride double with Dob," Win said, almost defiantly, "and go over the hill."

"Fine," Matt said. "Hop to it."

It surprised them, and himself, but it made him feel better. They knew now that, as far as he was concerned, Libby didn't need to hear of everything that went on.

Chapter 8

Libby had never seen Matt look so upset as he did that Sunday when he rode in from the wood ranch on the mountain in a driving October rain. She was at the cabin on the claim, her eating house at the lower landing closed since no steamers called on that day. Matt was much away, and she knew why, yet Sundays usually brought them all together in something that at least resembled a close family life. But that day it had looked as if he wouldn't show up. And none of them had really brightened up until eleven-year-old John, watching patiently at the window, let out a yell.

"Hey! There he is!"

The youngsters all hurried out to the dogtrot to greet him, leaving Libby behind and a little put out that her own undivided attention, that day, hadn't satisfied them. Yet she was smiling when Matt came in with her brood flocked about him.

She saw at once that something troubled and angered him. Yet he said nothing to explain it until he had visited with the children, showing an impartial interest in the doings of each of them. Then they ate Sunday dinner together, and this hidden mood of Matt's lighted a spark of itself in her. He was growing restive, and she couldn't help relating it to the hidden part of their marriage. She knew she hadn't been fair with him when he had given so much and asked so little.

She waited patiently until after dinner when, their excitement over Matt's being there subsiding, the children turned back to their other interests. Win, John and Pip went over to the boys' half of the double cabin. Letty and Margaret went up to the loft over this half, where they and she slept. It was as if the youngsters knew parents should be given a bit of privacy. They were too young to guess that everything between her and Matt had been arranged tacitly to give as little of privacy as possible.

And then, sitting by the fire together, Libby learned that it was nothing but the Indian trouble that exasperated Matt and disturbed him. It was something that had bothered her hardly at all. While there were danger signs, the military had recognized them and made preparations. After Major Hall's defeat in the Yakima, the Oregon governor had sent more militia into the interior. Major Rains, in command of the regulars at Fort Vancouver, had sent up three hundred additional troops.

The last Libby had heard was that a powerful force had been sent into the Yakima to undo the damage done by Haller's ignominious trouncing. Matt's annoyance and ill-concealed worry resulted from the way this had turned out. He had got back from Dalles City the day before, and before he left there word had come in that Rains' expedition had turned into an even greater fiasco than Haller's.

"They'll never get another chance like that," Matt fumed, "to settle it permanent."

Crossing the mountains in overwhelming force, Rains had come upon Kamiakin and his warriors forted at the gap between the Yakima's two valleys. They had learned later that Kamiakin, expecting the next trouble to come in the Walla Walla where a large militia force was gathered, had sent a good part of his warriors there to help the chief of the Walla Wallas. His stand at the gap had only been to gain time to hurry his women, old people and children off toward the Okanogan.

In fairness to the major, Matt said, Rains hadn't known that at the time. Even so, his caution was scandalous. His howitzer fire quickly knocked out the Indian breastworks on the hills, yet he refused to try to take the high ground.

A large number of troops, including officers, grew unable to bear the Indian taunts and rushed and took one of the hills, anyway. Rains ordered them back. His noncombatants by then away, Kamiakin simply ordered his braves to scatter in all directions, and that was the last contact with them. Rains went into camp until the steadily worsening weather gave him an excuse to return to Fort Dalles.

"How on earth," Libby gasped, "can he excuse that?"

"Oh, he's got an excuse," Matt muttered. "Cut and dried by old Wool, himself."

Libby nodded her head. General Wool commanded the military department of the Pacific from the comfort of San Francisco, but his attitude had filtered down to many of the regular army officers in the field. Foremost was his detestation of the civil militia on which the security of much of the frontier depended. He was a spit-and-polish, book soldier, and an old man. He had no taste for teaming his boys in blue with the rough, unlettered butternut soldiers and he made no bones about it.

"I suppose," Libby sighed, "that Rains was afraid to rely on the volunteers in his command."

"At least he'd say that," Matt agreed. "But mostly he was in no rush to get tied up in a long, rough job. Vic Trevitt told me he heard from an officer at the fort that Wool's asked for a heavy reinforcement of regulars. Enough they can launch a campaign next spring without the help of the militia."

"Next *spring?*"

"That's what the officer told Trevitt. Meanwhile we've got hostiles running everywhere and persuaded the army's scared of 'em."

"Well, I don't blame you for being annoyed. But we're safe enough down here."

"Yeah," Matt said quickly. "Sure we are."

He agreed too readily, leaving Libby herself depressed. Surely they were safe, so far from the scene of hostilities. There were the soldiers at the middle rapids blockhouse and encamped at the upper landing. By now there were at least fifty civilian males working on the portage, or for Matt in his wood business, or out on the land claims. Each day saw scores more of them pass through. That surely was enough to keep the local Indians quiescent.

She didn't want to think about it and said, "If there's anything I've learned out here, it's not to borrow trouble. It was such a good summer. For you, too, I know."

"Yes," Matt agreed. "I've done mighty well. And I've been thinking, Libby. We could afford to put up a real house now. Winter's not the best building weather, but it's my slack time. A couple of my woodcutters are good carpenters. They'd be glad of the winter work."

Libby was instantly wary. As far as the landing knew they were a real family, and for the past year Matt had talked of building them a real frame house. Surely they needed it. When he was home they were seven. Even when he was away the dogtrot bulged at the seams. While he had said that they could afford it, he expected to pay for it out of his own money. He knew hers was earmarked, now and for the next several years, for the education of her children.

It was typical of his generosity, but she couldn't abide the thought of becoming again indebted to him. She hadn't let him support her and her family except during the first awful winter. She had repaid him every cent of that from her own earnings. In her mind, if not legally, they had divided the donation land so that she owned the half-section where Alister rested. If he built a fine house for them, it would put everything back in one pot again, and it would create other problems. She feared that he was angling, because his feelings had changed, for a way to draw them closer and make him truly her husband.

She said in quick dismissal, "No, Matt, not yet. We don't know how long this boom will last. We'd best hold onto what we've laid by till we see."

He grinned. "I've ordered up the lumber, Libby. It'll show up one of these days on a scow behind the *Fashion* or *Belle*."

"Oh, Matt."

"So spend your spare time drawing plans of what you want."

"My spare time," Libby said faintly. She thought of her business at the landing. Of the schooling she kept up for her children in the evenings the winter long. Of the household that with Letty's help she ran. Of the cows, chickens, the big garden they had each summer. "Matt, can't you cancel the lumber order? I just don't think you should spend the money now."

"I could cancel it," Matt said doggedly, "but I'm not going to. The young 'uns are shooting up. They need space to grow in. They ought to have rooms of their own."

She feared he was thinking of a room for himself and her, at last, which was his right if he cared to insist. That first winter, when they had lived in the wagon box with a rough lean-to shelter attached, there had been no problem. They were so crowded together, intimacy would have been impossible anyway. When later they put up the cabin, Matt had, with a tact she had appreciated, suggested a dogtrot, a structure with its two halves separated by a bay open to the outdoors on one side. She and the girls could sleep in one half, he had explained. The boys could take the other, he with them so they wouldn't be nervous at night. It was the arrangement they still had when he stayed overnight, and one she didn't want to change.

She said hesitantly, "Where would we build it?"

"Well, this is a good location. Easy walk to the landing and high ground, with a fine view of the river." Also close to Alister's grave. She wondered if Matt had thought of that, too. He went to the window, turned and said, "Come over here."

Libby rose and went to him and stood looking out into the rainswept dusk. Below and slightly to the left was the lower landing, to which the portage railroad had been extended. Even in the gray light she could see the roof of her own small building, the wharf boat and the Bradford warehouses. Upstream was Gant Island, and in the other direction lay Strawberry. On the far side of the river rose the more precipitous Oregon Mountains. At their base was the landing Captain Van Bergen had just built for the *Fashion,* to compete with the Bradfords' facilities.

But Matt was speaking again: "If we put the new house

just in front of us here, the dogtrot would make a storage building. We could keep the same barn and corrals and your chicken house and garden patch." He looked at her inquiringly, and she had to nod her head. "We haven't begun to work the land yet except to crop the timber on the mountain. When ours is gone, I'll buy more on stumpage, and when that's gone we'll turn to grain and stock and maybe fruit. After all, land's what we came for and to farm it. We should bear that in mind when we build."

He was thinking in terms of years to come with everything pooled together. She knew she should tell him there could never be the reward he wanted for his long patience. It wasn't that she didn't feel his physical attraction. She was only thirty-two, he two years older, and she didn't deceive herself about the vague yearnings so often disturbing her. Yet each time she toyed with the thought of being no longer a fraud, something inside her contracted into a benumbed knot. Maybe if at some point he had insistently taken her, it would have been different. But Matt wasn't like that. He wanted her heart as well as her body, and the one without the other would not content him.

She said somberly, "Matt, I'm afraid I must tell you—" A flash of blackness in his face made her hesitate. She knew she couldn't destroy his hope without destroying the kind of man he was.

He said roughly, "Go on. Tell me what?"

Amending, she smiled wryly and said, "Well, that I'm not sure I could be happy as a farmer's wife. It's true that land was what we came for. I mean Alister and I. But that was because a law practice can be lean pickings on the frontier, and our family was large and growing. Here you and I've run into opportunities we never dreamed of. By buying stumpage or government timber, you can keep your wood business going indefinitely. It looks like I can keep on feeding travelers as long as I want. And there's Win to send out to school, then Letty and John and Margaret and Pip. It's taken me all this time to get myself started, and I'll be another year getting the money laid by to send off Win."

"You know I'd send them."

"It's something I've got to do myself, Matt. And since I can't be a real housekeeper for years, I don't think you should build that house."

"The lumber's coming, and a house there'll be for the young ones."

"All right, Matt."

She knew that even so she had destroyed something that had long sustained Matt: the chance of their becoming at least a working team instead of running their separate businesses. In this, too, she had rejected him, and her heart wept, and she knew she must somehow put an end to her fraudulence. He might have intended to stay the night and maybe several days with the family, his slack time having come. But he didn't stay long after their conversation, giving a little more time to the children and then heading off into the arrived night for the wood ranch on the mountain.

It was Win's eyes afterward that nearly undid her completely. He'd had an exciting summer working for Matt in his wood business. It had been a mistake to let him, for ever since he came home he had been different. He seemed to have lost all interest in the books that once had absorbed him. He seemed to resent something about her personally. She knew the changes had come to him that gave him some of a man's wanting. Had they opened his eyes to her sham with the man he had come to look upon as he had once looked upon his father?

Guilty and thus made stern, she set them all to their studies. She helped them when needed but only then. They had good minds and had to learn to apply them for themselves. The evening wore away, and finally they had all gone off to bed, and she was restless. When the cabin was thoroughly quiet, except for the popping of the fire and rattle of the rain, she bundled herself against the weather and slipped out of the cabin.

The wind hit her, and she braced herself against it and walked off across the open ground toward the slight rise where so much of herself had been laid away forever. She could see the twinkling lights of some of the other cabins at the lower landing. And then she came to the iron fence around the small plot of ground and looked across it at the granite headstone brought up from Portland.

For a long minute she could say nothing, and then, "Alister? He wants me. He's earned the right to me. But I can't."

She waited with rain beating into her face. For what? For him to release her from her promise? No. He had not asked for the promise. She had given it, and nothing within her had changed. Yet still she waited, for sometimes when she was there she had the sense of a response coming to her out of the void. Yet that night there was only her confusion and the troubledness Matt had stirred in her.

And then it came as clearly as if Alister had spoken. She was not a fraudulent wife but a faithful one. To this man whom she had married for all time. She and Alister had found their land here, although it had cost him his life. She was still determined to live the life they might have had together, to bring up his children as he would want.

Chapter 9

Framed, roofed and with its false siding in place, the new house cut off the view of the river. Libby couldn't help frowning when she came out of the cabin behind, on her way to her day's work at the landing. She had always taken pleasure, when she stepped out her door, in the picturesque sweep of the river below, the islands and farshore mountains. Matt's house had appropriated this unto itself, blinding the cabin and demoting it already to the status of an outbuilding. She couldn't help resenting his stubbornness about building it. Adding to her faint displeasure, the boys were already over there, their interest in the work making them indifferent to the dry cold of the December morning.

Libby turned along the path to the landing, but this took her by the end of the new structure, and Pip saw and yelled at her.

"Hey, Ma!"

Libby ignored him, instantly moved from her mild crossness to outright annoyance. No matter how often she corrected him, he fell more and more into the settler children's way of talking.

His childish voice called almost mockingly, "Mother!"

She turned, then. His seven-year-old body was framed in an opening cut for a window on the upper floor. She could hear hammering and sawing somewhere behind him. She said coolly, "What is it, Pip?"

73

"Come see the stairs they put in. Now you can come up here on steps."

"That's fine," Libby said dutifully, "but I haven't time now. You can show me later."

Pip's face fell. She knew he had watched for her, hoping to show her the latest in the undertaking that had absorbed everyone but her. She nearly yielded, but he deserved a reprimand for the flippant way he had first addressed her. She turned and hurried on along the path, made again aware that The Cascades was claiming her children, just as the place had claimed Alister.

She had taken the first step toward preventing that when she declined to place them in the school that the other children attended. She had contributed money, and knew that Matt had given even more, for the three-month winter term each year. Snobbishness had had no part in her wish to supervise the schooling of her own youngsters, herself. The common school, so crowded and so brief, could give its students little more than a passing acquaintance with the three Rs. Her own children had to have infinitely more than that.

Yet, to be truthful, there had been bias involved, as well. While she knew Mose Biggers hadn't contributed a penny to the school's support, Amy and Dob were going there. She suspected that Matt had arranged for their admission when he made his own gift of money, and that was all right. She would deny education to no one. But she couldn't tolerate Win's and Letty's being thrown so much together with their counterparts in that family.

Libby reached the landing and felt better, for there she could lose herself once more in the hustle-bustle of a busy day. The *Belle,* sister of the upriver *Mary,* would be in shortly before noon. At about the same time the *Fashion* would tie up on the far shore to connect with the *Wasco* above the rapids. They would all bring passengers to patronize her eating-house, each of them, before he had cleared The Cascades, good for a dinner and supper and a breakfast on the following morning.

The landing seemed almost deserted at that hour of the morning, but Libby knew that Bradford men were busy at the wharf boat and warehouses. A couple of soldiers from the blockhouse at the middle rapids were over there, loading a light wagon with commissary stores. Her own place stood across the portage tracks from the wharf. It was plain and austere due to the undressed lumber from the upper landing sawmill from which it had been built.

Molly Macabe, who worked for her, had already opened for the day's business. Libby saw that she had already swept and dusted and built fires in the kitchen range and the heating stove in the dining room. Only a few of the long tables were covered with fresh, bright cloths. That was all they needed at this time of year when travel was cut down by winter weather.

"Morning, Miz Cowan," Molly called cheerily when she heard Libby come in. She was already peeling potatoes in the kitchen. Libby returned the greeting and joined her there before Molly asked the inevitable question. "Well, how many mouths are we fixing to feed this trip?"

That was always a matter of guesswork. While the freight that passed over the portage increased steadily, passenger trade fluctuated, especially at that time of year.

"Make it thirty," Libby said. "Which means we'll get forty or twenty, as usual."

"Well, we can manage. We always do."

Libby smiled, for Molly had been priceless help. She was young , blond contrast to her own darkness, and very pretty. That was no minor point, for between them they made a decorative feature that didn't hurt the all-male trade a bit. Yet this surfeit of male admiration affected Molly no more than it did Libby. She was married happily, although childless, her husband working with the Bradford crew that at present was building a new trestle up by the middle rapids.

Libby put on an apron and fell to work, for they had too much to do to indulge in much conversation. She prided herself on offering variety, as well as quality and quantity, a not too common attitude among those on the frontier who made it their business to feed travelers. Much of the provisions had been produced by her, with the children's help, while the boats weren't in. Beef, ham, bacon, and sometimes lamb and even wild game, came from settlers out on the claims. But the potatoes Molly finished peeling were from Libby's own garden. So were the canned vegetables, the pickles and piccalilli. The eggs came from her own chickens, the butter and cream from her own cows. The light bread, pies and cakes were of Molly's baking in the intervals between boats. The rest came from the Bradford store at the upper landing or had been ordered up by boat from Portland. The work and care had paid off, for her meals had become part of the pleasure of the river passage to and from the interior.

They were ready when a steamer sounded down the river, sending ahead its long, heavy blasts. At that point Win and Letty arrived to help in the rush about to start. Presently the *Belle* slid into view to vanish again on the river side of the wharf boat's huge deckhouse. Her gong rang out, and almost as if thus summoned, the portage cars backed onto the wharf. They brought freight and passengers from the *Mary,* and only moments later men from both boats were streaming over the tracks and into the eating-house.

It was a scene grown very familiar, and Libby saw she had guessed the day's trade very well, for the *Fashion* and *Wasco* passengers had yet to ferry across from the far shore. She didn't care what boat they were from as long as they ate her food, liked it, and paid for it at fifty cents apiece. It kept her and Molly busy refilling dishes, platters and coffee pitchers, for the tables were soon filled. When the room began to empty, Libby stood by the door to collect. She was pleasant with all of them, even those who gave her the eye and sometimes a bold leer. Then it was over until suppertime, when it would all begin anew.

Matt came down with the younger children, and they all ate leftovers. Then Matt hurried back to his carpenter work, taking his charges with him. Letty and Win helped clear the tables and then with the long job of washing dishes that both of them loathed. But it was part of their training, and Libby insisted that they do their part. Afterward Letty went home while Win stayed to split wood for the kitchen range.

Libby sat down with Molly for more coffee. They had another meal to prepare and serve that day, and she was already tired. There was a stack of coins on the table in front of her, which she studied with thoughtful eyes.

"Twenty-one dollars," she reported. "I didn't miss it by much."

"Come another summer season," Molly said, "and you'll be rich."

"Not rich. But I'll have enough to send Win off to school in the fall. That's all I want."

Molly regarded her thoughtfully. She said hesitantly, "It's none of my business, Miz Cowan. But are you sure it's what the boy wants?"

"Of course it's what he wants." And then, feeling oddly uneasy, Libby added, "Why did you ask a question like that?"

"He's sure taken with the steamboats. Look." Molly tipped her head toward the front windows.

Libby turned her own head to see Win moving swiftly toward the door of the wharf boat. He had sneaked around the building and gone over there. He had made friends with the *Belle*'s crew, she knew, and they let him come aboard. She said with a frown, "That's natural in a boy his age. He'll outgrow it."

"I expect," Molly said, although she didn't seem convinced. And then she said sharply, "Do you feel all right?"

"I feel fine. Why?"

"You're flushed."

"I'm just a little tired," Libby confessed. Surely that was all that made so many things rub her the wrong way. "I seem to have got up on the wrong side of the bed this morning."

"If you don't get more rest, there'll come a morning when you can't get out of bed at all."

"Nonsense."

Molly wasn't to be put off. "I mean it. Ever since I've known you, you've drove yourself without mercy. It worries me. You're close to the limit, Miz Cowan. Either you lower your sights and get more rest, or you'll wind up nowhere at all."

Libby said crossly, "When do I have time for more rest?"

"You can take time. Clara Barton would be glad to help me with supper and breakfast in the morning. That'd give you a couple of days before the boats come up again, and I wish you'd do it. Go home right now and pile into bed and just take it easy."

It was odd that the suggestion should be so appealing. She said in sudden weariness, "I don't know, Molly. Maybe I will."

Molly's smile was swift and sunny. "No maybes about it. You do it. Clara and I can handle things here."

"I know that. All right. I will."

It was the first time since she had started west with Alister that she had surrendered to weakness. She didn't agree that it was as serious as Molly made it out. But she *was* tired, and it was making her short with the children and Matt and generally out of sorts. She had no intention of going to bed, as Molly suggested. Extra time with her family would be just as restful, and good for them all.

Molly herself went home for a couple of hours in the afternoon before returning to help prepare and serve supper. They dampered the stoves, locked the building, then went their separate ways, Molly up toward the middle rapids where she lived. Win hadn't reappeared from the steamboat, and Libby decided to have a friendly talk with him that night about his future. Walking up the path toward the cabin, she remembered that she had promised Pip to take a look at the stairway in the new house. She would show great excitement over it, and whatever other work Matt and his men had accomplished since her last inspection.

She expected to find Pip at the construction work, but he wasn't in sight, nor was John. She looked in to see that Matt and his men were busy on the second floor. They didn't notice her, so she went on to the cabin. She had barely opened the door there when her plan for a relaxed holiday with her family was swept from her. There on the bench before the fireplace fire, Letty sat chatting happily with Amy Biggers. They turned their heads to look at her, startled and guilty because they hadn't expected her home.

Libby regained enough poise to say coolly, "Well. Hello, Amy."

Amy tipped her head stiffly and said, "Good afternoon, Miz Cowan." There was nothing of defiance in her manner, and yet nothing of humbleness.

Libby hadn't forgotten how once she had admired the girl and had been touched by her and her lot. Nor had she cut her cold on sight, as she had the others in that family after their enormous treachery and desertion. On the other hand she had never been more than coldly civil to Amy, as she was now. For Amy was one of them, tainted by Mose's blood, and in the end that was bound to tell.

Letty said in a small voice, "What brought you home, Mamma? Are you all right?"

"Of course. I just decided to take time off."

It was so without precedent that Letty probably thought she was checking up. And it terminated the cozy chat for, with surprising dignity, Amy rose to her feet. Libby was grudgingly impressed by her grace and budding beauty, even in her faded calico dress and heavy, cowhide shoes. When she cut Letty an unconscious comparing glance, she saw a begging look in her daughter's eyes. The child wanted her to be gracious and tell Amy to stay. Libby refused, turned quickly away and went on to the kitchen. She heard voices too low to make out. A moment later the door opened and closed again, and she went back to Letty.

She didn't like the look in the child's eyes and said aggressively, "She knows she's not welcome here. So do you. And you both know why."

"I don't know why!" Letty said stormily. "It wasn't Amy and it wasn't Dob who did what you hate!"

"Don't shout at me, young lady," Libby warned. Yet something had contracted in her chest. Letty, too, was becoming a young woman and a very pretty one. This spunkiness wasn't like her at all. "They're all peas from one pod. I've forbidden you children to associate with them, and you've disobeyed me."

"Well, it's not the first time," Letty flung at her. "I talk to Amy every chance I get and to Dob. So does Win. They're not like that miserable old man and Toby."

"I'll be the judge of that," Libby said crisply. Win, also? She thought of Amy's promising beauty, and her heart contracted again. That was something else she would have to talk with Win about. If there was much of the father in her, Amy could be the ruin of the boy.

She changed her clothes, then went out to feed her chickens and gather the eggs, her thoughts of rest and relaxation dismissed. Her children were like mercury drops that, no matter how you tried to get hold of them, went gliding away from your fingers. She didn't want to be with Letty in their present moods and lingered to clean the hen house. By the time she was done, John had come in with Pip. They had been up along the slough on whatever adventure. Matt knocked off work on the house, and his men left. He asked no questions about why she was home on a day when the boats were in. He must have talked with Letty. Then Win showed up, unapologetic, and he and Matt went to the barn to milk. Letty had started supper by the time Libby went back indoors. She had been crying, for her eyes were swollen and red.

Libby let her go on with the meal. When Win and Matt came in with the milk she strained it into pans and put it in the cooler. The other children were aware of the tension that charged the cabin and saw a partial explanation in Letty's face. Libby's exasperation spread to Matt. He must have seen Amy come home with Letty. His cool eyes informed her that he was on Letty's side—which was Win's, also, since he, too, had been disobedient. Matt lighted the lamps, and presently they sat down to a supper in which silence and mute contention reigned.

Afterward Libby set her children to their lessons as inflexibly as if she had not previously planned a holiday with them. Then, as he always did when he was there, Matt helped her do up the dishes. Finally she listened for a moment to the quiet of the other room, then said in a low voice, "I know what you're thinking. But it's too much to ask me to forgive those people. Any one of them."

Matt had never spoken to her in such a cool, clipped way. "Who asks it? Not me? I only hoped that by now you would have voluntarily."

"Why should I?"

"If not for your own sake, then for the children's. The young don't hold onto a hurt or a love like you." He drew a slow breath. "And maybe like me."

She said miserably, "Oh, Matt. I don't want to be at odds with you. We never have been. But I've got to do things my way. It's the only way I can."

"I know that."

"Bear with me. Please?"

"You know I always will."

He hung up his towel and presently went off into the night, as he had taken to doing more and more on evenings when the children studied. Often, she knew, he walked up to the blockhouse, for he had made friends with Sergeant Kelly. Again he would go to some bachelor's cabin to talk, spin yarns and perhaps play cards. Sometimes this bothered her, for it announced that he had no real fireside, no wife to grace his evenings and share his bed. Yet that evening she was relieved to have him gone.

She sat with the children, and when they had studied she heard their lessons one by one, sending each to bed when he was through. When at last she found herself alone with Win, she tried to regain the relaxed and friendly mood in which she had come home. He had a history book open on the table before him at which he scowled. All at once she reached and closed the book, smiling at him.

"I won't make *you* recite tonight," she said indulgently. "There's history and there's also the future. Let's talk about that." He was so instantly guarded that she lost confidence but rushed on, anyway. "You don't know how like your father you are, Win. How well do you remember him?"

He said uneasily, "How do you mean?"

"Well, you were pretty young to realize how fine he was. And what a splendid mind he had. And how proud he was of you. He had great plans for you, Win. For your brothers and sisters, too, but for you especially. You're so much like him, and he knew that even when you were very young."

She saw that she was reaching him. He had adored Alister too, and when she broke off, he said, "What kind of plans?"

"I thought you knew."

"For me to be a lawyer? I thought that was your idea."

She realized that through some precocious insight he understood her need to bring Alister back to life through this flesh and blood that was so like him. He was resisting it, and that left her no choice but to bind him by shifting the desire to Alister, who had never actually expressed it.

"You were too young, of course," she said quietly, "for him to have said definitely what he wanted for you. But he loved the law. He wanted to practice it here on the frontier and eventually to go into politics. He'd have gone far. Maybe he'd even have become governor or a senator. I'm sure he'd like for his son to go on from where he had to leave off so cruelly. I know I would. Don't you think it would be a fine thing for you to do?"

"Yeah," Win said. His eyes were moist "Sure I do."

"Good." She bent and kissed his brow. "By next fall there'll be money enough for you to start. Maybe down to one of the valley academies for a year or so. Then east for the law. That's why I make you study so hard." She smiled in gentle chiding. "And why you mustn't waste time fooling around the river and the boats. And with youngsters your age. Especially girls."

Chapter 10

Through the loft window Amy could see her father lurching off toward the barn, shabby boots scuffing the frozen snow. A while ago she had heard a familiar sound, to which she awakened on many mornings, that of bickering, intense and bitter, downstairs. She knew Mose wasn't setting out, now, to do the morning chores at the barn. That would be left to her and Dob. He was on another toot and heading for the jug he kept hidden there. The jug was his horn of plenty. Once it had given him courage. Now it fortified him against a wife who had grown shrill and shrewish since they came to The Cascades. Even the patient Sarah had had enough of him.

Amy watched Mose stagger into the barn, then lifted her eyes to look on into a frozen and beautiful world. Snow had come with the turn of the year and had fallen with hardly a letup for three weeks. With it came temperatures lower than anyone remembered, intensified by a steady wind. It had produced an undreamed-of effect, now that the air was clear and the wind down. The river had frozen, in places from shore to shore, until nothing moved between The Cascades and Portland, or between the upper landing and Dalles City.

It was strange not to see the *Fashion* and the *Belle,* yet other excitements had taken their place. The sloughs made excellent skating, if you owned or could borrow skates. Sledding, too, was a lot of fun. Even the grown-ups had come to regard the interlude as a pleasant pause in the busy rounds of their lives. Mose Biggers had looked on it as a good excuse to get himself tight as a tick.

Amy heard sounds beyond the hanging blanket that separated her half of the attic from Dob's. She turned her head, careful to keep the comforters snug at her shoulders. The loft's only heat came skimpily from the flue that passed through, and the air was cold. She heard the noise of Dob's quick dressing. Then the end of the blanket pushed back, for the ladder opening was on her side. Dob looked over at her and saw she was awake. He came in and sat down on the edge of her bed.

His light brown hair was rumpled, and she thought his sleep-puffed face was, in its way, as handsome as Win Arlen's. He grinned at her lazily. He spoke in a voice lowered so it wouldn't be heard by their mother downstairs. "What're you going to do today?" It was Saturday, and there would be no school.

His air of conspiracy made Amy say with a grin, "Nothing I don't have to."

"I mean fun. After we get done with the work."

Amy's eyes brightened. She was sure now that he had something exciting up his sleeve. "What are you going to do?" she countered.

"Matt Cowan knocked off work on the house and made a big bobsled. You know? The kind you steer?" Amy nodded her head. "Well, I seen Win yesterday. He told me him and some of the others're taking it up on the hill today."

Amy frowned. "What's that got to do with us?"

"Win asked me to come." Dob waited teasingly a minute. When she refused to take bait, he studied the ceiling and said vaguely, "Seems to me he said something about bringing you, too."

"Golly," Amy breathed. "His ma don't know that."

"She won't be there. You want to come along? They'll be up there all day."

She wanted to go. She had seen neither Letty nor Win since that unhappy afternoon when she had been come upon by their mother in the Cowan cabin. That was weeks ago, but the memory was still painful. She said, "Maybe I will and maybe I won't. You better go down, now, so I can get dressed."

"Seems to me you've got mighty modest."

"I've grown up."

"That what's started pushing out your dress?"

"Don't get fresh."

Dob didn't mean anything by it. Usually they were close and understanding, yet he liked to tease and to make her out for such a child. She was framing a retort about his scraggly whiskers, but he went over to the ladder and disappeared.

She dressed quickly, her teeth chattering, then dropped down the ladder, which bottomed in the kitchen. Dob had already sat down at the table to eat the same old breakfast of cornmeal mush and soggy biscuits. They kept chickens, but the eggs had to be sold at the Bradford store or to one of the portage families. They had cows, but there was no butter for the biscuits. It, too, had to be sold. They fed hogs on skim milk and slop, but at butchering time there was never anything for the family table but sidemeat. When a cow calved and the calf grew into veal, it became something that would bring in money.

For those were things Sarah could do, with Dob's help and Amy's. The farming Mose did on the section of free land he had gone to such lengths to claim brought in next to nothing. If he planted grain in the fall, it froze or drowned out or produced a crop too skimpy for anything but pasture. He knew how to raise corn, but most of that went into cow feed or hominy, and not a small part into the still he had up in the timber. There was never more than enough hay to carry the other stock through the winter. He'd tried sheep at first, but most of them had died or been killed by wolves or coyotes from the mountains, so there was no wool to sell. About all he marketed was some beef steers he ran, they requiring little work of him. It was the same with Toby on his adjoining half-section, where he lived with the lazy, fat hog of a wife he had found down the river.

No wonder Sarah looked so defeated, all-gone and

querulous. Amy glanced at her, finally, and said, "Morning, Ma."

Sarah, preparing a churning, grunted something unintelligible, for there was no love lost between them. Amy had never forgiven her, anymore than she had Mose and Toby, for their cheap cheating on the Arlens. And that couldn't hold a candle to their outrageous treachery and desertion. Now there was the disgrace of it she had to share because they would never live it down.

Amy ate quickly and was through by the time Dob was. They took pails and went to the barn to milk and do all the other morning chores. She expected to find her father, keeping company with his jug, but he wasn't there. Gone over to Toby's, probably. His son and daughter-in-law spoke his language, and he was comfortable in their company.

Milking old Elva, Amy wondered how sinful it was not to honor her father and mother, a disobedience of the gospel that she couldn't help. Something had happened to her, back there, as damaging as what had happened to Libby Cowan, although Libby would die before she would concede it. As soon as she was old enough she would get away, and she didn't much care in what direction. Likely it would be with some man. She wasn't blind to the way their eyes lit up, the soldiers, travelers and even some of the settler men, when they saw her. She wasn't ignorant of what went on in their thoughts. Mose and Toby were too foul-mouthed for there to be much she hadn't learned about. She could make out, all right, as soon as she had a little more age and courage.

It was because of this steady hope of escape that she had been glad when they started the school. And, of course, when it turned out that she and Dob could go even though Mose had refused to put up any money. She had a quick, receptive mind, and it was hungry for learning, not just how to read and write and figure but for the kind of things the Arlen kids studied.

She and Dob finished milking and took the milk to the cabin. Afterward, while Dob cleaned the barn, Amy fed the hogs, the chickens, and gathered the eggs. The horses

were running loose now, or there would have been even
more work. Amy wondered how they were faring with all
the snow on the ground. Probably they had gone up into
the timber where there was more shelter.

Before they went back to the cabin, the work done, Amy
said, "What time are you going to the sledding?"

"Soon as I can get ready," Dob answered. "Win said
they'll bring lunches and build a great big fire. You coming?"

Noon was one of the problems in Amy's mind. Eating
cold biscuits smeared with grease while the others had big
lunches was bad enough at school. But there she couldn't
help herself unless she wanted to go hungry all day. She
shook her head. "Guess not. Before this afternoon, anyhow."

"Win said especially to bring you."

All at once there was a stinging in Amy's eyes. "Tell
him maybe I'll come over this afternoon."

"Come on." There was concern and understanding in
Dob's eyes. "We're as good as anybody there."

"Are we, Dob? Aren't we cut off the same bolt—" She
tipped her head toward the cabin. "—as them?"

"I don't know about that," Dob said fiercely. "But I
know this much. I'm going to plough my own furrow."

"Me, too," Amy said. "But you go on. I'll come later."

"Promise?"

She thought a moment and sighed. "Yes."

"Well—all right."

Dob had a defiant way about him that Amy envied but
could never duplicate. He changed out of his barn clothes
into things not much better. He fixed a couple of biscuits
and put them in the pocket of his shabby coat. He dug out
an old stocking cap. When Sarah, who had finished churning and was working the butter, asked where he was going
he said he was going to knock around a while. She didn't
really care what either of them did, and his explanation
satisfied her. Dob gave Amy a secret wink and was on his
way to the sledding.

Suppressing a sigh, Amy turned to her mother. "Can I
work that for you?"

" 'Bout done."

They certainly weren't good company, so Amy climbed the ladder to the loft, which had gradually warmed up. The thing about Sarah she had never understood was how she could rail and rant at Mose, as she had done in private that morning, yet never say a word against him to anybody else. Maybe it was a matter of memory and sentiment. Or, more likely, a matter of saving what shards of pride she had left. Or perhaps Mose had become a cross she gained some secret reward for bearing the way she did.

Amy got a book Win had given her, undoubtedly without his mother's knowledge because it was a school book he had once used. It was a grammar, and she had gone over and over it, trying to weed the Biggers way of talking out of her own. It was hard, for even when she understood what the book said, habit was strong and the tongue slipped easily. She settled down with it.

She studied past noon, and the downstairs grew quiet. When she descended to the kitchen it was to find that Sarah had left, maybe to go over to Toby's, too. Amy ate cold biscuits hurriedly in the welcome privacy of the kitchen. Then she got into her coat, scarf and stocking cap and slipped away from the house.

She knew where to go and struck off across the claim at an angle. That would take her toward the footslope of the mountain where they were sledding. It was a long walk, and while she moved briskly her feet grew cold. The soles of her shoes were worn so thin she seemed to be walking barefoot on the frozen snow. Eventually she saw the smoke of a fire. Soon after she could hear the outcries of the sledding party. She hesitated, almost losing her nerve. But in a moment she went on.

When she came to the foot of the run she lost her uncertainty and grew excited. It was a long run, starting steep and fast and leveling gradually onto the big flat. It had been used so much that forenoon that the snow was packed hard. It seemed to her that nearly every young person at the lower landing was up by the bonfire at the top. Even as she climbed toward them, the big bobsled started down.

She stood at the side, moving her feet excitedly up and down, while the sled loomed down upon her and whizzed past. It was long enough for half a dozen to ride at a time, the front runners separate and fixed for steering. Dob was on this part and went by so fast he probably didn't notice that she had kept her promise. The others sat behind him, each with a crosspiece to support his feet, leaning forward and with his arms locked to the person ahead. It looked great fun, and her eyes shone with eagerness to try it.

She watched the sled speed on to the end of the run, well below her. There the passengers piled off to take the rope and haul the sled all the way back to the top of the hill. She turned and climbed on up the slope to the fire. She was pleased when Letty left the group and came to meet her, smiling a welcome. Amy's wary eyes informed her that there were no grown-ups present.

"Hello, there," Letty said, holding out her hands. "I'm glad you came, Amy. Come to the fire and get warm."

It helped Amy to toss off her returned shyness and uncertainty. Win stood at the fire, warming himself. He sent her a grin and lifted a mittened hand in greeting. There were others there less inclined to make her welcome. But it was Win and Letty's sled, their party. When they went out of the way to be friendly, the others smiled and nodded to her, too. No one in the world could be nicer than Win and Letty Arlen. After all, they weren't responsible for their parents, either.

The sled made it back to the top of the hill, three boys pulling the rope, three girls laughing and trudging along beside them. Dob grinned at Amy, and she knew he was glad she was there. Her heart warmed with love for him, too. Win took the steering rope from Dob and grinned at Amy. "Come on. You ride behind me. And hold on tight."

"That's the whole idea," some boy yelled. "To get the girls to hug you."

Dob grinned and said to Letty, "And you behind me."

"Don't mind if I do," Letty said and smiled back.

Ralph Engels and Edna Sharp claimed the last two seats. When they were settled in place, the other boys gave them a big push, and away they went. The sled picked up speed until the runners sang on the hard snow. Amy had never gone that fast and could hardly breathe. The wind blew against her lashes until she could barely keep open her eyes. An odd, not unpleasant sensation attacked her stomach. Dob had his arms around her from behind. In a minute they were streaking and bouncing so that she forgot herself and threw her arms around Win. It was the first time she could remember when they had really touched each other. She felt so happy she pressed her cheek to his back and let the wind shut her eyes.

All too soon the sled leveled out and slowed down. She lifted her head and opened her eyes. Yet on and on they went until finally they came to a complete standstill. Arms and legs untangled, then they all stood in the snow, exhilarated and eager for more.

"Were you scared?" Win asked with a laugh.

"Some," Amy admitted. "Not enough to make me holler."

"I think it would take a lot, "Win said, "to make you holler, Amy."

That pleased her so much she hugged it to her heart all the way back to the top. Three more couples claimed the sled and went swooping down to the bottom. Amy stood by the fire. Her hands were frozen, for she owned no mittens. But she was ashamed to hold them out to the heat and let their rough-skinned redness declare her poverty. She remembered what Dob had said, that morning, about ploughing his own furrow. He was better equipped for it than she, but she was more determined than ever to plough one of her own. It didn't matter what she had to do. She would improve her lot and earn the right to hold up her head.

Chapter 11

Libby bore with poor patience the period in which the *Belle* and the *Fashion* were kept away from the lower landing. Yet when the ice broke up at the end of January and they returned to service, they brought her little cheer. The boats and portages were busier than ever, but it was with army freight being pushed to Fort Dalles. The army was launching its spring campaign earlier than anyone had expected. It had forbidden newcomers to the interior and advised those there to get out. So there were hardly any passengers to patronize her place of business, and she had to look forward to a slack summer at a time when she needed to prosper.

The first warning had come in late January, when a Colonel Wright and ten new companies of regulars had gone up to Fort Dalles. Wright was to command the expedition, and he made no bones about it being a long and difficult undertaking. On the heels of the new regulars, five additional volunteer companies went up the river as well. Added to the troops already up there, it made a tremendous force. It didn't seem to her that the thousand hostiles said to be making trouble up there could stand very long against it.

Few others at the portage shared her opinion, and there was uneasiness all about. This wasn't lessened when in early March the *Wasco* was fired on by Indians from the shore while it was passing the mouth of Dog River. On the

91

heels of that, the *Mary* was hailed from shore by a settler who had been driven from his cabin by Indians. He identified them as Klickitats and Yakimas, the known hostiles, and they had been in considerable number. It showed that they had moved south from their regular haunts, as Matt had said all along that they would. It put them much too close to The Cascades, and a cry went up for the army to reinforce its detachments there.

So all Libby could do was gasp that Monday, March 24th, when Matt came storming into the eating-house where she and Molly had put in another exasperatingly profitless day. She thought from his red face that he was about to have a stroke. When she cried, "Matt! What is it"? he didn't seem able to answer.

Then he hauled in a long breath and said bitterly, "I knew it! I said it time and again! Leave it to old General Wool and his San Francisco dunderheads!"

"Leave what?"

"Our safety. That's what."

Molly, who had been more of a worrier about the Indians than Libby, said in a small voice, "What's he done now?"

"I'll tell you what!" Matt said in an angry roar. "Instead of putting more troops here to protect us and the portage and military stores, like we expected, they took what soldiers we had!"

Libby felt a flutter in her heart. "Took all of them?"

"All but a measly squad under Kelly at the blockhouse. The rest left on the *Mary* this morning to help in the campaign."

"Heaven help us," Molly breathed.

"We better fix to help ourselves," Matt retorted. "Libby, I want you to take the youngsters and go down to Portland on the *Belle* tomorrow and stay there. My advice to you, Molly, is do the same. Them Indians know how important this portage is to the army and how defenseless we've been left. It's my feeling they'll lose no time taking advantage of it."

Libby felt her flesh crawl, less from the danger Matt saw than from the idea of giving up everything voluntarily for perhaps the whole vital summer. It might put Win's leaving off an entire year, and after the sledding party she had heard about she knew he must see as little as possible of Amy, that Letty must follow him off to school as soon as it could be financed.

"Oh, Matt," she protested. "You've talked about that kind of trouble all winter. Now you've got so you see Indians behind every rock."

"I'd rather see 'em where they aren't than not see 'em where they are."

"Wright doesn't seem to think there's any danger. Or he wouldn't have let the troops be pulled out of here, Wool or no Wool."

Matt looked at her somberly. "Well, as you've never let me forget, they're your children. And it's your life." He went stomping out.

There was an odd expression around Molly's eyes. She hadn't missed Matt's dig, and it angered Libby that he should have given their private affairs an airing before her. Then Molly said quietly, "He's right. I don't know what got into the army, but they've sure made us sitting ducks."

"Are you going to take his advice and leave?"

Molly shook her head. "I'll take my chances. But if I had children—"

"Nonsense. I'm not going to tuck tail and run at the first Indian scare."

"I hope that's all it is," Molly said with a shrug.

They closed up, parted, and Libby started home. But instead of going there immediately, she turned off the path toward the plot of ground enclosed by the iron fence. When she reached it, she only felt her spirits sink lower still. The roses she had planted there so long ago looked lifeless and unlovely under the weepy sky.

She hesitated about speaking, but at last said. quietly, "Alister? I don't want to endanger our children. But is Matt right? Ought I to leave you and everything and take them away a while?"

Each time she came there it was harder to evoke an answer from the great mystery he had entered. It seemed as if his spirit had left the place to which she was pledged, a thought unbearable. Then all at once she felt the strength flow back into her body. Her mind eased and her heart lifted. He was speaking thus, telling her not to be afraid. That was all, but it was much. She lifted her eyes from the sodden earth to the leaden sky, and there seemed to be light behind the clouds. She let the corners of her mouth crease in a small smile. She wished she could tell Matt that his fears and the realities were far apart. Alister would know, for his spirit was still with them and had powers denied the living. She walked back to the main path and went on toward the new house.

Matt had let his workmen go but, as he could, he had been painting the house, the last step before it would be ready to occupy. A room for each of the children upstairs, a single bedroom down. He had never said he intended to live there instead of at the wood ranch. But if he did? Well, there would be Win's room after he went away, which was all the more reason for him to go. The older children already knew that she had remained faithful to their father. She felt so encouraged by her visit to Alister that she wanted to make peace with Matt, but he wasn't working at the house. She went in and through all the rooms, but he wasn't there.

She went on to the cabin to learn from Letty that Matt had gone up to the wood ranch, taking Win along. He had left word for her that they would be gone overnight, it being late when they started.

"What for?"

Letty shrugged. "He didn't say, and I didn't ask."

Libby frowned. There were numerous things that took Matt up there now and then. But it was a study night, from which she never excused the children, and Matt knew that as well as Win did. She stared into Letty's eyes, which had seemed to her to be sullen ever since the quarrel over Amy Biggers. Win seemed to accept the idea that he must follow in his father's footsteps, but otherwise he was as silent and withdrawn from her as Letty. And now Matt? Was this intentionally added to the dig about having nothing to say about the children? It was something she would take up with him and Win both on the morrow.

She grew sure of Matt and Win's joint defiance when the whole of the following day passed without their returning. That, too, wasn't unusual for Matt, but in Win it was inexcusable. On top of that, her feeling of well-being diminished somewhat when she saw the *Belle* and then the *Fashion* slip off far below. When they were at their moorings there was a feeling of being in touch with the world outside. Now they were gone, and the landing would be isolated until they were back again. Her man and nearly grown son were off God knew where. And there were no soldiers, anymore, except for Kelly's nine men at the blockhouse, which was quite a ways upstream.

When night came with the absent still missing, Libby grew less angry than worried. She and Letty did the chores once more. They sat down with the three younger children to a silent supper. While they had a study period afterward, even Libby had little heart for it. The situation reminded her too vividly of a night long ago. The night she and the children had arrived at the landing, half dead from walking over the mountain, to find everyone vanished into thin air.

John and Pip were nervous about going to the other half of the dogtrot to sleep without at least Win there. That told Libby they had Indians on their minds, too, for they had slept there by themselves without complaint while Win had worked for Matt that summer. Libby shamed them into it, and when they had gone, Letty looked at her mother with a frown.

"You can't blame them. All the kids are talking about having to fight Indians."

"A game."

"Well, why haven't Matt and Win come back? Matt said just overnight."

"If you must know," Libby said with a sigh, "Matt and I had a spat. He's angry. And you know how Win's been too big for his britches now for months."

Letty turned and followed Margaret up the ladder to the loft. Libby banked the fire, trying to ignore the trembling that had started when Letty openly admitted her own fear. She blew out the lamps and climbed the ladder, knowing she would go up to the wood ranch herself the first thing in the morning. If they were all right they would get a piece of her mind. And if they weren't—

Daylight still didn't come very early, even with March so nearly gone. Libby awakened in a gray, drizzly dawn and remembered what she had set herself to do. She slipped from bed and down the ladder to build up the fires in the fireplace and kitchen stove. She dressed in the growing warmth of the open fire. The children, trained to meet the new day without having to be rolled out of bed, began to appear. By the time they had done the morning chores and eaten breakfast, it was after eight o'clock. When John and Pip had gone over to make their beds and clean their rooms, and Margaret was doing the same upstairs, Libby told Letty quietly what she intended.

"I'm sure there's nothing to worry about," she said with false confidence. "But don't let the boys run all over today. Make them stay in sight of the cabin. It's quite a walk for me. I might not get back in time to come here before I have to go to the landing." How good it would feel, she thought, to have the packets there again.

Letty nodded, unspeaking, and Libby started out, bundled against the weather. From the distance she could see that the Bradford men had already started work at the wharf. Smoke rose peacefully from distant cabins, giving the lie to the fear of trouble. She made her way to the muddy road that went over the mountain. For a while this followed the river. Then it angled off to the north, passing at a distance the settlement and blockhouse at the middle rapids.

She had nearly gained the road when a horse and rider cut into it from the west at some distance ahead of her. Libby frowned when she saw that the rider was Amy Biggers, forking the horse like a man with her skirts up to her knees. It was a school day, but apparently she was going to the upper landing. The burlap bags behind her were full, probably with butter and other truck Sarah traded for staples at the Bradford store. If Amy recognized her, she gave no sign, turning the other way and digging her heels into the ribs of the horse. She pulled quickly ahead and out of sight.

Soon Libby herself was angling off from the river and toward the mountain. The trees and brush about her dripped from the lazy rain. The soft footing was a far cry from the frozen earth of January. She walked briskly, rehearsing what she would say if she found Win and Matt to be on a holiday at the expense of her nerves and time. Then all at once she heard a sound that startled her, for it was like no sound she had ever heard at The Cascades.

She stopped, her mouth open. The memory of the sound pulled her head in the direction from which it had come, which was toward the river and behind her. It had been like the sound of an axe biting into a log, except sharper and more carrying. She walked on, puzzling, and in a couple of minutes it came again, that time wheeling her half about.

The howitzer at the blockhouse?

While she knew she was guessing, her knees nearly buckled. She walked on in slow steps, hardly halfway to Matt's cabin. When the sound came again, she was sure. The intervals proved the blockhouse cannon was being fired as fast as it could be loaded. It was never fired for practice or ceremony. It was there for defense, nothing else. It was firing now in anger and in earnest.

She hung in suspense between her fears for her children, left behind, and for Win and Matt, supposedly on ahead of her. If the latter had run into trouble, it would have been a full day ago. That would have kept them from returning home at the announced time, and there would be nothing she could do to help them. She turned back and went flying down the muddy grade of the winding road, feeling miles away from the children she should have stayed with.

The howitzer fire continued at spaced and menacing intervals. Presently she could hear something else that was unmistakably the firing of rifles. When that drenched her last ember of hope, she let out a wild cry.

"*Alister?* You told me—!"

She fell silent, rushing on. She had only voiced her own

desires there at his grave, and Alister had told her nothing. She had endangered her children out of her blind selfishness. Now she had deserted them at the very time they needed her. She tried to run faster but could not.

She was nearly out of the timber when a heavy male voice yelled at her with an urgency that couldn't be doubted.

"Miz Cowan—for God's sake! Over here!"

She nearly went headlong but stopped and turned. Linus Biddle and Ira Jastrow stood at the edge of the brush, motioning frantically. When she saw the blood streaming down the side of Biddle's face, she turned to plunge wildly on for the landing. They bounded after and caught her, holding her by the arms.

She screamed, "Let me go—my children—!"

"Miz Cowan, they're all over the place down there! It's too late! You'd never make it to your young 'uns alive."

They were good and decent men, but she hated and fought them. Yet they dragged her hurriedly into the concealment of the timber.

Chapter 12

When Amy first heard shooting she had nearly reached the upper landing. Her first wild impulse was to whirl the horse and go streaking for home. In the next shallow breath she realized she would be no better off there. The danger was everywhere. She had been lucky to get over the mountain unmolested.

She rode quickly off the trail into the dripping brush. Then, after a moment's hesitation, she slid to the ground. She tied the horse to a tree, started to remove the crude saddlebags to take with her, then reminded herself that she would be lucky to save even her life. The firing in the distance was heavier by then. She thought she smelled smoke. She had to know what she faced before she could tell what to do.

Leaving the horse, she walked swiftly to her right along the timbered slope of the mountain. Four years at The Cascades, and a naturally roving spirit, had taught her the lay of the land quite well. In only a few minutes she came to a place where she could see down over the bluff. The angle was too flat for her to see down to the landing itself. That delayed her for only as long as it took to locate the tallest tree, swing up into it and climb as high as she could.

All at once she had a view that made her blink. Indians lay all along the bluff top below. They were naked, smeared with red clay, and had white streaks slashed across their faces. Some of them seemed to be looking on, but most were shooting down into the landing and settlement. Smoke and flames farther on told her the sawmill was burning. Her stunned eyes moved on to see that the *Mary* was under fire that came from the brush beyond the creek. Men on board were shooting back. Only the upper story of the log store building was visible, but the Indians on the bluff seemed to be concentrating on it. There was no shooting across the river, but she could see white men racing about the *Wasco,* which was tied up over there.

She seemed to have a mouthful of dry paper, and her shocked eyes stared until they stung. But the scene began to grow remote. Her problem was herself, a thirteen-year-old girl caught alone and cut off from her kind. She could stay hidden high in the tree and hope she wasn't found. But she was too close to the bloodthirsty savages to consider that. She might try to hide herself deeper in the timber, but that would leave her still alone with Indians skulking everywhere. In spite of the shooting, the places below where there were people of her own kind drew her like magnets. She began to work her way down to the ground. . . .

The trouble at the upper landing had started only moments before Amy's arrival, an obscene intrusion upon a scene of the usual midweek serenity. The *Mary* and the *Wasco* had come in from Dalles City the afternoon before. Since loading would take most of the next morning, the fires in both steamers had been allowed to die down. Lawrence Coe, who now ran the store for the often absent Bradfords, had opened it for business. A crew building a trestle and warehouse on one of the offshore islands had gone to work. So had the crew that ran the sawmill, and yet another crew had headed off down the portage tracks with the mule cars. In the settler cabins wives and mothers, breakfast over, had settled to housework as on any other day.

The first shooting came from the bluff. It was intended for a diversion, for other Indians waited in the brush at the lower level. The first volley brought shrieking whoops from the latter, and they came swarming in on the settlement. The first to die was a family caught in a cabin, a man, his wife and her young brother. All three were shot down, scalped, dragged to the river and thrown in. The next objective was the sawmill where the surprised, unarmed workmen could only make a dash for the store. All but one made it, and the one was shot down and scalped.

Captain Baughman of the *Mary* had been ashore with one of his men. He saw instantly that the Indians' intention was to capture the steamers and burn them, preventing a call for help from reaching Fort Dalles. He went charging toward the steamer, but the Indians were in ahead of him, and he and his man were driven back into the timber. Three others of the crew, working at the wharf boat, braved a storm of bullets and sprang aboard the *Mary*. Already on board were Hardin Chenoweth, the pilot, who was in his cabin, and Buckminster, the engineer, was on the boiler deck. Two others, John Chance and Dick Turpin, had been idling below.

At the first shots the defenders managed to get hold of such firearms as the packet afforded: a revolver, an ancient dragoon pistol, and a rifle. Turpin grabbed the rifle and jumped down into a flatboat alongside just as the first Indians reached the gangplank. Before he could do any good a bullet took him in the shoulder and knocked him into the river to drown. Chance managed to reach the hurricane deck, where he was hit in the leg, and was able to drive the Indians back from the gangplank. At that point men who had reached the store began to shoot back. The attackers of the *Mary* were driven back, but only into the brush, and they continued to pepper the packet with angry lead.

On the boiler deck Buckminster threw cordwood into the firebox as fast as he could move. The trouble was, the wood racks were all but empty, the fire had been out, and the water in the boiler was nearly cold. Even if they kept the packet out of hostile hands, he didn't know if he could build steam enough to back out into the river. Even if he did, the Indians would never let them put in at Cowan's woodyard and take aboard the fuel needed for the thirty-six-mile run to Dalles City.

Up in his cabin, Chenoweth was biting his nails. Captain Baughman was clearly cut off, so the responsibility was the pilot's. If the settlers could be collected and got aboard, and if he could get steam enough to reach the woodyard and refuel, the *Mary* might save those on this side of the river who were still alive. Yet without plenty of steam the packet could easily be swept down over the rapids and pounded to bits on the rocks, drowning the lot.

Chenoweth made a run over the hurricane deck and reached the pilothouse without being hit. But immediately glass began to fly from the pilothouse windows. He dropped to the floor. The thin walls of the superstructure were poor protection, but they made him impossible to see and difficult to hit. He yelled down the speaking tube to Buckminster. Between them they decided to try to get away, make it to Dalles City and bring back soldiers from the fort. If they failed, maybe the *Wasco* could do it. By then she, too, was under attack on the south shore. . . .

In spite of the shots and blood-chilling yells echoing off the cliffs, Amy had been drawn ever closer to the landing. The rain had tapered off and stopped, but the woods that helped conceal her were drenching wet. First she had come down to the upper creek, waded across and slipped into the farside woods. From there she saw the sawmill, a little downstream from her, and it was burning like a dry haystack. She crept on, passing an empty cabin. She thought that if she could reach Matt's woodyard she might find someone there, and the ricks of wood would offer places to hide. But when she drew near it, she saw that it, too, had been put to the torch. She turned and moved blindly in another direction, and all at once she nearly keeled over in a faint.

Behind trees below her, two men stood watching the river. They were dressed like settlers, and one wore a boat cap. Otherwise, she couldn't have been sure they weren't Indians who hadn't painted up to go on the warpath. She ran toward them, nearly crying out in relief. While they had no weapons, they were company. Because of the racket, they heard her only at the last moment and whirled around, instantly dangerous. The one in the cap was Captain Baughman. He was outstanding at The Cascades, so she knew him. To him she was only a shabby, badly frightened settler girl to worry about, but he motioned her to them.

He smiled when she reached them, but his voice was low and intent. "Well, young lady. Where did you pop up from?"

Amy told him in a voice so breathless she could hardly talk. Feeling safer, she could think at last of the lower landing. Of Dob and Letty and Win, of the others she knew and liked, and last of all of her father and mother, Toby and his wife, Stella. She added in a small voice, "Is it like this all over The Cascades, Cap'n Baughman?"

"I'm afraid it is. There's a mess of Indians mixing it up. Too many to be all locals. They aim to seize the portage and hold it and cut off Wright's big army in the interior before he can even get started on his campaign."

"Then it looks pretty bad for us, don't it?" Amy said faintly.

"Well, we've got nothing to cheer about. You keep yourself hid, now, and watch. We might have to cut out of here any minute."

Amy pressed to the blind side of a tree and tried to shut her ears to the ugly uproar. From time to time she heard one of the men make some low comment. She paid little attention until she heard the captain say, "From the stack smoke, Buckminster's getting some steam. Not that I know what good it'll do. The savages'll cut Chenoweth down like a stalk of corn if he tries to take the wheel."

A little later the other said, "Something's up! They're chopping loose the line!"

Amy's heart sank, for she thought he meant the Indians were setting the *Mary* adrift to go down over the rapids. When she dared to look, she saw that white men on the boat were cutting the lines. But there was nobody visible in the pilothouse, where the big steering wheel was. A moment later she saw that the near side-wheel was turning slowly in the water, just the same. The *Mary* began to ease away from her moorings, bringing a screeching protest from the Indians.

In a moment Baughman said in awe, "Neatest trick I ever seen. Chen's handling the wheel from the floor, where they can't target him."

Amy gasped, "How can he see?"

"Somebody's giving him instructions through the tube."

Baughman was so pleased with his pilot he seemed to have forgotten there were murdering Indians all around them. Amy couldn't forget that, but she also watched the *Mary,* which might give them the only chance they had to stay alive. In a moment she saw the paddles bite into the current and begin to haul the packet around. Her whistle let go in a defiant blast that drowned the angry yells of the Indians, and Amy's heart nearly jumped out of her chest.

"Into the bushes!" Baughman said sharply. "Fast!"

They barely made it to denser cover when Indians from the lower level came racing and yelling past them. They were on their way to keep the *Mary* from salvaging enough wood from the burning yard to make it to Dalles City. When the last of them had gone by, Baughman got to his feet.

"We'll never get a better chance to make it to the store! Come on!"

He grabbed Amy's hand, and they went racing forward. At the edge of the woods Baughman stopped to wave his cap until he was seen by somebody at a store window. The man there nodded and motioned for them to come on. A moment later every gun in the store seemed aimed at the cliff top in a covering fire. Amy found herself flying at the end of Baughman's arm, the other man pounding behind them. Two or three times, while they crossed the open ground, she heard the snap of a bullet passing overhead. They reached the front of the store, and a man lay there dead. Amy recognized him: Jim Sinclair who had worked for the Hudson's Bay Company when it ruled the country. There was blood all over his buckskin shirt. She saw this flittingly, and then she was being pulled inside the store.

Even as this happened, a shout went up inside. A man at

a window overlooking the river yelled exuberantly. "Old Chen fooled 'em again! Instead of heading for the wood-yard, he went across the river! They're taking on rails from a fence over there!"

Amy remembered Captain Baughman's saying they had nothing to cheer about. They did now, for not long after the *Mary* got away, the *Wasco* put off upstream and stopped to take aboard what was left of the rail fence. Somebody said she had picked up a number of settlers from the south shore and workers on the portage over there. Somehow a surprising number from the north shore had made it to the store, as well. They were mostly women and children, and most of them had run through a curtain of gunfire the same as Amy and her companions had. But Amy knew the size of the settlement and how many must still be caught somewhere outside.

Weak, dazed and half sick from the burned gunpowder that charged the place, Amy seemed all but forgotten. She wanted to be, for even here she couldn't forget that she was a Biggers. The women and children sat on benches against an inside wall. While she stayed with them, she tried to pretend that either she or they weren't there. This was hard, particularly to keep her eyes off a young mother whose baby laughed and gurgled in its unawareness of the danger. Amy saw, also, that the men and older boys were giving their entire attention to the defense. They had been helped in this by the fact that their rough, crowded fort-ress happened to be a well-stocked store. There had been weapons and ammunitions on hand already. By chance a shipment of army rifles and ammunition had been pass-ing through, and it had been appropriated, too.

The store's only stairs were outside, making it impos-sible to climb that way to the upper floor and gain a bet-ter outlook and increased field of fire. But the men had taken down the stove and enlarged the hole the pipe went through. With a ladder, that made it possible to man both floors. Now they were drilling gun holes on both floors with braces and bits. Indian bullets had about shat-tered the windowpanes, which were dangerous shooting positions at best. As gun ports were made, iron shutters were put on the windows. This darkened the interior but made everyone feel better.

Amy ran her eyes over the merchandise on the shelves and counters. After the skimpy pantry at home, the food-stuffs there had always fascinated her. She knew they wouldn't go hungry before the steamers got back with troops. Yet she had barely taken comfort in this thought when a child complained of thirst and was told by its mother to hush, that there was no water. Amy knew it was too dangerous for anybody to try to slip out to the river for water, at least before dark.

The hope inspired by the escape of the steamers, and of being at last with other settlers and behind log walls, kept draining away. With the steamboats escaped from their clutches, the Indians turned their full attention on the store. Amy heard somebody say the men who had been working on the warehouse were still trapped on the island. One of them was dead and several others wounded. A woman voiced another worry that she had kept to herself until then. Her husband had heard from a trooper being transferred to Fort Dalles that Colonel Wright planned to move out on the campaign at once. That opened the dis-heartening prospect that the soldiers might have left Fort Dalles before the steamers reached there.

Not long after that an alarm came down from the upper floor. The Indians were managing to hit the roof from the bluff with firebrands: burning pitchwood, faggots of burn-ing straw wrapped around rocks, even pieces of red-hot metal. Somebody rushed down for an axe, and somebody else yelled for water. But there was no water, so they be-gan to dip brine from a pork barrel and take it rushing up the ladder. When Amy heard the sounds of chopping, she winced. Each blow meant another hole in their secur-ity. Almost by the minute, afterward, they heard the thump of stones landing on the roof. The women grew silent, and for some reason the baby began to whimper.

It went that way through the long afternoon, the men fighting roof fires and shooting through the gun ports. The women sat with strained faces, and now and then one of them took herself and children into the wareroom behind the inside wall. Amy had to go dreadfully but couldn't bring herself to follow their example. Lawrence Coe passed out food and ale from the store stock, but Amy found she couldn't eat anything. She drank her small ration of ale, for she was very thirsty. It was so bitter she could hardly swallow it. They all waited for night, when one of the men would try to get water from the river.

That hope, too, was dashed. At nightfall the Indians began to burn the cabins. Some of them got over on the island and set fire to the warehouse. It lighted the landing like day, preventing any sortie, for water or for escape. Then one of the men fighting to put out a roof fire exposed himself too recklessly and was shot, to fall dead to the upper floor. That didn't faze the other firefighters, and before long two more had been hit. Amy knew by then that nothing could save them, and she no longer much cared.

She didn't know she had gone to sleep, sitting on the bench with her head against the wall, until something awakened her. There was a stir of excitement on the lower floor. A breed boy who had lived with the dead Sinclair had slipped down the chute that connected the store with the wharf and got back with a bucket of water. Knowing how far it would go among some thirty parched throats, Coe took charge of it, rationing out a half dipper per person.

He was a tall man with a handsome black mustache that looped down past the ends of his mouth. Better educated than most of the settlers, he had always seemed aloof to Amy and to hold himself a notch above the rest, as well as her. Yet after he had given her water, Coe paused for a moment. He didn't exactly smile, but something in his dark eyes seemed kind and concerned.

He said quietly, "Keep your chin up, Amy. People have come through worse than this."

Amy hadn't realized he knew her name. She nodded and managed to thank him. He went on, and she puzzled about why he had singled her out for a word of encouragement. She wondered if she had had friends at The Cascades besides Letty and Win and Matt Cowan.

Chapter 13

Sergeant Kelly was a blocky man of fiery complexion and an even more fiery temper, and there was considerable he could find fault with that Wednesday morning. Considering that its purpose was defense of the lower settlements, the army had built the blockhouse in about as unlikely a place as even the army could have found. It stood on a low, flat point of land at the head of the middle rapids, between the river and the portage railroad. The river there was so narrow a strong boy could sling a rock across to the Oregon shore. The steep, brushy slopes on both banks made excellent positions for the potential enemy that had now become a most undeniable reality.

Such room for building as there was had been taken up by the blockhouse and its outbuildings and the portage tracks. The closest settlement was an Indian village a little downstream, and then the cabins of a dozen or so Bradford employees. Three-fourths of the settlement the sergeant was responsible for protecting, after the big detachment was removed from the upper landing, was either two miles down the river or four miles in the other direction.

Even so, quite a few had made it to the blockhouse, since the brush could conceal friends as well as foes, and gained admittance by braving a storm of bullets. At the moment Kelly was listening to this shooting and the return fire from the loopholes on the upper floor, and shaking a hysterical woman by the shoulders while he yelled.

"You listen to me, Miz Cowan! There ain't a settler here who ain't got somebody caught outside the same as you! Just you simmer down, like they have, and let us get on with our business! You hear?"

"I—I'm sorry." Libby nodded her head, all at once feeling weak and ashamed. She should have known he wouldn't let her go, anymore than Biddle and Jastrow had been willing to, up on the trail. "It's just—"

For a moment Kelly's face lost its fierceness. "Believe me, Miz Cowan, I know how you feel. But everything's been done that can be done at the lower landing by now. You couldn't help your young 'uns. You'd only get your ownself killed. Maybe that don't look so bad to you, right now, but if they come through they'll need you."

Libby nodded, although his philosophy was beyond her grasp. Kelly went clomping up the stairs to the loopholes and men shooting from them. A refugee woman sitting on the puncheon floor looked up at Libby with sympathetic eyes.

"Don't fault him, Miz Cowan. He's doing his best with what the army give him to do with."

Libby nodded. As far as the settlers who had made it there were concerned, Kelly's best had been good enough. The Indians' first move had been to nail him down by opening their attack on the blockhouse, which would let them have their way with the rest of the settlement. Their opening fire had dropped a soldier, badly wounded, in the blockhouse doorway. There were only five others there at the time, including Kelly, and three soldiers had been caught somewhere outside.

The sergeant's answer had been to haul out the howitzer, hoping it would put the fear of God into the savages long enough to organize a defense of the lower settlement. The first round dispersed a party of Indians trying to set fire to a storehouse. As he had expected, the shot had less effect than the fiery roar of the weapon, magnified by the slopes. A second round had dispersed a war party gathered to fire at the blockhouse from the Oregon side. Those now inside owed their lives to the little cannon. It had confused and driven back the Indians long enough for them to make it in. These included, besides Libby and her unwelcome escorts, the men who had been working on the portage trestle and some of the families from the closest group of cabins. Then, all too soon, the Indians lost their awe of the sound-belching demon and closed in again. Now small-arms fire from the loopholes was all that held them off.

A woman's voice snapped, "Set down, Miz Cowan! You're giving us all the willies!"

"I—I'm sorry."

Libby halted her restless pacing, which had been unconscious. The firing positions were all on the upper floor, where the sleeping quarters were, and the lower floor had been used by the detachment as a kitchen, dining room and storage place. The benches had been taken and jealously held, so she joined the women sitting on the floor. She knew they weren't short on worries, themselves, even those with no children caught outside somewhere. The blockhouse hadn't been heavily stocked with food and ammunition. What water there had been for the use of the handful of soldiers had vanished. The wounded soldier, who had been taken upstairs, was in great pain and now and then a groan escaped him.

The day wore away, and night brought a development none of them could have guessed. For some reason the hostile shooting slacked off. Libby heard a man say that such as there was came from the Oregon side of the river. On the heels of that there came a heavy rattling on the door, which was locked shut by a steel bar. A man resting from his turn at the gun ports hurried over and called through. Then he opened the door and a wounded soldier—one of those caught outside—stumbled in. He reported that for some reason the Indians on their side of the river had withdrawn. That had let him make his way to the blockhouse from his hiding place.

Kelly and the other men went into a quick huddle. Libby's heart sank when she heard one of them say the Indians had probably weakened the attack here to strengthen one somewhere else. They talked back and forth, then

Kelly explained his decision to the women. He and some of the men were going to make a sortie to try to pick up food and ammunition from the nearer cabins and bring in what wounded they found. In only a few minutes, half a dozen of them had slipped out the door and were gone.

The idea that came to Libby, not long later, was born full bloom. It was dark as a cave inside the blockhouse, and most of those on the lower floor seemed asleep. There was still shooting, although desultory, both on the floor above and from the far side of the river. Men had brought water from the river, and she rose to her feet on the pretext of getting a drink from the pail on the bench by the door. Her movement seemed to stir no other. She put her hands on the heavy bar guarding the door. She could lift it. But before she had done so it came to her that the door would have to be fastened again from the inside or an Indian could slip in. She hesitated for only a moment.

Creeping across the floor, she came to a sprawled figure. Her hand found a shoulder and shook it gently. The figure stirred, and a groggy, feminine voice muttered, "What—?"

"I'm leaving," Libby whispered. "You'll have to bar the door again."

"Miz Cowan? No—don't—!"

"Shush."

Libby turned quickly, freed the door and slipped outside. For a moment her legs felt too weak to move, then she drew a deep breath, bent over and ran across into the brush. She half expected to be grabbed and scalped immediately, but there seemed only the empty growth and night about her. She moved quickly to the portage tracks, reaching them at the upper end of the trestle. Freed of branches and tripping roots, she ran.

She had crossed the trestle before she realized she was exposing herself badly for the sake of speed, and the Indian village wasn't far ahead. Still moving rapidly, she turned off the track and got up on the slope so she could pass behind the village in the concealment of the timber. The trees weren't dense there, but the floor beneath them was rough and foot-tangling. The rapids were then below her, the place where Alister had died.

And now his children might have died and joined him in the great mystery because she hadn't respected Matt's warnings. She sobbed and went rushing on and got by the village, which was so dark and quiet it seemed deserted. Only a few minutes later she began to hear gunfire and went half out of her mind, for it came from the lower landing. In moments more she saw the first bright, dancing daubs of fire down there.

The Indians were burning the lower settlement, and there were still white people alive there or there wouldn't be so much shooting.

Libby went on mindlessly, although there was nothing she could possibly do but get herself murdered. When she came to the wagon road that went over the mountain, she could see that nearly every building at the landing was in flames. She could do nothing but pray that Letty and the younger ones had somehow got away and found refuge. She stumbled to a halt beside the road, sick and frantic. In the next breath the darkness up the road produced figures coming toward her. Half fainting, she darted from the road, dropped to her hands and knees and crawled into a thicket. Several Indians went by at a jogging trot, all but naked, and all of them armed. They seemed to have come off the mountain and were heading for the landing.

She lay on the wet moss under the brush, weak and whimpering. It wasn't for herself. Only involuntary instincts had moved her into hiding. She knew that her younger children had perished. Before that Win had been lost for some mysterious reason. Her mind had dwelt on the younger ones, for Win was with Matt, or he had been, and not alone in the face of the furies. She crawled out into the open and stood up. She had no wish to return to the blockhouse and thought then of Matt's wood ranch. She might at least find out what had happened to those two whom she had also failed so miserably. She struck off toward the mountain, not caring if she met more Indians or that she was already half dead from exhaustion.

The apathy that settled on her thereafter made time pass quickly. She didn't come out of it until again she heard shooting in the distance. It was like blinking awake because of sudden noise, and she stopped and looked about. She was well up the mountain and nearly at the side road that went off to Matt's wood ranch. The shooting was nothing like that which her ears had grown used to, but it persisted. Her mouth dropped open, and she saw a glimmer of the truth. This strengthened and hurried her, and instead of going on to Matt's lane she cut directly into the timber. She was certain by then that the shooting was at his cabin. Maybe they had just been caught there and pinned down. The thought that they might still be alive pumped new strength into her.

Wary as an animal, she crept toward the cabin through the thick timber. Branches slapped her in the darkness and once she tripped and fell. The ground was open about the cabin, barn and the several small outbuildings. She crept to the edge of the clearing and stopped, trying to study out the situation in the dark. There was shooting from the cabin and, she thought, from the barn as well. The Indians were firing back from scattered cover closer in than she was. She stood with her cold arms clutched to a breast in which the spark of hope grew stronger.

She moved slowly until she was at a rear angle to the cabin and the woodshed just back of it. There didn't seem to be any Indians at that point.

Gathering breath, she cupped her hands to her mouth and screamed, "Win! Matt!"

She knew that, having betrayed her presence, she had to make it to the cabin or die on the way. They must have received other stragglers, for all at once other guns opened on her side of the cabin to give her cover. Her legs flew, and she knew she was being shot at when a bullet snapped past her ears. She heard a piercing shriek, saw a naked figure race toward her, but all at once it gave a bound and fell. Somehow she got in between the cabin and woodshed. A man dashed out, grabbed and speeded her inside. She heard a voice say, "Ma'am, you're danged lucky something drew most of 'em away from here." Then she fell in collapse on the kitchen floor, not fainting but all gone inside.

She was conscious of hands lifting her, then found

herself in a chair. There were no lights, but she had grown used to the darkness and could see the figures of men at the glassless windows. There were several refugees, and there had been a long fight here. Her eyes searched the obscurity and found Win just as his voice choked, "Mamma—Mamma—!" He pulled her head to him, gentle fingers stroking it and her cheek.

It seemed a long while before she could say, "Matt?"

"He's—well, he's here."

Ice formed on her heart. "He's—?"

"Just hurt, Mamma. But pretty bad."

Libby choked back a sob, not knowing why she should be so grateful that a second man hadn't been taken from her life, strange though their union had been. She said, more calmly, "Where is he? I want to see him."

"He's—well, not conscious."

"I still want to see him."

"You might as well know." Win's voice was frayed and tired. "He probably won't pull through. He was shot in the chest and bled so much and went so long without help—"

Something had happened to Win. He kept holding her to him and stroking her hair, his body hard and strong and full-grown. He had become the third man in her life. She knew he wanted to know about the rest of the family and how she happened to be there alone, but feared it would only upset her if he asked. It was something she couldn't bring herself to tell him until he did ask. She sat in the chair, hearing the shooting, knowing it was the concerted attack on the lower landing that had drawn away some of the Indians here. The ones she had hidden from on the road had been part of them.

There was something they both could talk about, and she said, "What happened to you?"

He told her. Matt hadn't said so, when they left the lower landing Monday afternoon, but his suggestion that they go up to the woods had come from his sense of what was about to happen. There were no firearms at the cabin at the landing. While he pretended to be only on a routine visit, what he really wanted was the two rifles, with ammunition, he had left hidden in the cabin at the wood ranch.

They had fully intended to return the next morning, for Matt expected trouble to break out at any minute. But a chain of events had interfered. Deciding to check on his horses while he was here, Matt had gone out in the last of the day, leaving Win behind to cook their supper. The only thing unusual about it was that he had taken with him one of the rifles.

Night had come on, Win said, without Matt's coming back. At the end of another two hours without his return, Win had been deeply worried, afraid he'd had a fall or otherwise been hurt in the dark. Win had only a general idea of where the horses would be found but, taking the other rifle, he had set out in that direction. He had gone at least a mile toward an upland meadow when he came upon Matt, crawling, crawling, crawling toward the cabin. It had been no accident. Matt had been shot. He had been since dark trying to get back.

He was nearly gone from the wound and shock and loss of blood and could hardly talk, so Win only questioned him enough to learn that Indians had done it. Later, before Matt lost consciousness, he'd said enough for Win to grasp the situation. Matt hadn't found the horses, for in the last light he had all but blundered into an Indian camp hidden in a canyon. Its very secrecy told him that it was hostile, compelling him to creep in closer. The minute he saw the stripped, war-painted figures everywhere about, he knew he had to get a warning to the settlements. They weren't Cascades, they were Yakimas and Klickitats from the hostile country inland. He figured the number at that one camp at about fifty.

Matt tried to sneak away, only to learn that he had already been discovered, for a shot came in from somewhere and hit him. It had dropped him, and only the brush and fading light had saved him. He had rolled into a thicket while the Indian camp exploded, still holding onto his rifle and prepared to make them pay for his life. Some of them had come almost close enough to step on him, but somehow they had passed him by in the growing dark.

Later he had crawled through the brush until he had put some distance between himself and the camp, which was still in a hubbub. He knew they were plotting something that a premature warning to the settlements would ruin. He knew he had to give the warning, and kept crawling, too weak and dizzy to stay on his feet.

Having found him, Win helped him back to the cabin. Matt had no concern for himself and tried to get him to go back to the landing immediately with word of the discovery. That Win refused to do before he had given Matt such attention as he could. And then, before he was ready to leave, the Indians had figured out where Matt might have come from. They weren't ready to fight, which could have betrayed their presence there to some passerby on the road below. But they had fired a couple of shots to let it be known they were there. Win had fired back from the windows to tell them they would get a fight if they tried to come in. They didn't know how badly hurt Matt was, so Win changed position with each shot he fired.

It had been that way all night and through the next day and night. The Indians weren't willing to pay the price of rushing the cabin. They didn't need to, for they had only to keep those trapped inside pinned down until it was time to start the massacre. Early the second morning the hostiles slipped away. By then Matt had lost consciousness, and Win knew it was too late to warn the settlements. All he could do was try to help Matt, and there was little he could do toward that.

Win had learned from refugees, later, what was taking place all along the river. These were men caught away from their homes and cut off from them. At first they had all taken to the timber. Then each in turn had thought of Matt's cabin on the mountain. It seemed too isolated for the Indians to bother with. There would be food there and possibly other people who would think of it as a refuge. Singly and in small groups they had arrived until now there were eight of them. That had all happened in the forenoon, and in the early afternoon a number of Indians had returned. Their purpose was no longer to keep their plot from being exposed. Mass murder had become the objective, and there was a goodly catch of white men in the cabin.

"But we're almost out of ammunition," Win concluded. "I guess you didn't help yourself much coming here."

"Oh, but I did," Libby said.

And at last Win asked the dreaded question. "The others?"

"I don't know. But I'm afraid—"

He clapped a hand over her mouth. "Don't say it. As long as you don't know there's hope."

"Yes." She nodded somberly. "Where is Matt?"

"In his bedroom."

Libby rose and went in there, more settled in spirit than she had been since the start of the uprising. A man with a rifle stood at the bedroom window, but he paid her no attention. She went to the bed and stood beside it, staring down at the vague, large shape.

"It's Libby, Matt," she whispered.

The man at the window fired a shot into the outer darkness. The smell of powder and blood and fever was strong in the room. She listened to Matt's breathing. It was shallow and fast. She slid a hand under the blanket and found a limp wrist. The pulse was as weak as the breath and very fast. Fear clutched her heart, and she smoothed his hot brow, pushing back the long, tangled hair.

Slipping back to Win in the other room, she whispered, "Is there water?"

"Yes. We got some indoors before the Indians came back."

He helped her put cold water in a wash pan. She tore up a clean dish towel and washed Matt's hot brow. Afterward she wet the cloth again and laid it across his forehead. No spirit of belated love had come to her. It was the first time he'd ever had a desperate need of help that she could give. She kept putting cold cloths on his forehead. The shooting she had listened to all day no longer impinged on her ears. She kept tending to him until her movements became sluggish. Then all at once she keeled over beside him, for the first time sharing a bed with him.

Chapter 14

Letty's first awareness of trouble came when she heard Molly Macabe's urgent voice cry out on the blind side of the new house.

"Miz Cowan—Miz Cowan—!"

By the time Letty had opened the door, John and Pip had popped out on the other side of the dogtrot, where they were still straightening up their room. She knew their nerves were as jumpy as her own because of the Indian talk, Matt and Win's mysterious absence, and now their mother's leaving them. Molly came rushing around the end of the new building. Her hair streamed, her face was red, and she must have run all the way from the landing.

She looked at Letty and then the boys and said breathlessly, "Where's your mother?"

"She went up to the wood ranch—" Letty began.

"Wood ranch?" Molly threw up her hands. "Oh, heaven help her!"

Letty's heart seemed to stop. "Mrs. Macabe! What *is* it?"

"Indians—blockhouse—haven't you heard the cannon?"

Letty remembered having heard a far, faint sound that had puzzled her but was too softened by distance to concern her. She said weakly, "You mean it's—the uprising?"

Molly kept gasping for air like a fish pulled out of the water. She swallowed, waited, then spoke more coherently. "They've got the soldiers hemmed in, and they've

118

killed some settlers! Soon as they've finished Kelly's squad, we'll have them down here on top of us! Oh, holy mother!"

The blockhouse was so far away, Letty said disbelievingly, "How do you know?"

"My man cut loose a portage mule and got away! He's gone to warn as many others as he can! I come to tell you folks! How long's Miz Cowan been gone?"

"About half an hour." All at once Letty saw the truth of it and the danger her mother had blundered into. Her stomach wrenched, and she cried, "Oh, no, Mrs. Macabe! *No!*"

Margaret, who had come down from the loft, began to cry. It brought a wail from Pip, and John was on the verge of tears. It served to remind Molly that she was the only adult there. With effort she wiped the fear lines off her face, although she couldn't take the look of it out of her eyes. She said briskly, "Well, you all get your wraps. We haven't much time."

"But where can we go?" Letty faltered.

"The river. They'll try to get the women and children off in boats, my man said, if there's time."

Letty was still in the grip of shock, but she hurried the younger ones and got her own coat and stocking cap. Yet go off and leave her mother there at the mercy of the Indians? And Win and Matt? She pulled to the cabin door, then numbly followed Molly, who was hurrying off around the new house with the younger children. Letty knew there were boats along the banks and in the back sloughs: catboats and keelboats, skiffs, bateaux, even log rafts. Molly could take the young ones off to safety, if anybody got away at all. She could manage without Letty.

Just beyond the new house, Letty turned quietly and ducked into the brush by the trail. When she looked back she saw an unsuspecting Molly rushing on, pulling Pip and Margaret by the hands. John trotted behind. Turning again, Letty moved farther away. Then she began to run in the direction her mother had taken when she left the cabin. She was a swift runner and strong. She could catch her and bring her back to the landing in time to get away on the boats.

Presently she could see the landing, and the excitement that had been stirred up there. People were running toward it from the cabins all around. She saw children who would have been at the village school and was glad that the word had reached there. Across the river there was a lot of scurrying, too, so the news had got over there. Then her own racing legs had taken her beyond this view. She kept hearing the blockhouse cannon, so the Indians hadn't killed the soldiers yet. Maybe her mother had been where she could hear that, too, and had turned back. Letty sucked in more air, hoping to see her mother coming toward her at any minute.

Then somebody behind her yelled urgently, "Letty—Letty—wait!"

She stopped, whirling, and there, racing after her, was Dob. He looked angry, and when he came up he said gustily, "Where do you think you're going, Letty Arlen?"

"To get—my mother—!" She was so out of breath she could say no more.

"You'll get yourself killed, you little idiot!" Dob grabbed hold of her arm. "Come on!"

She tried to pull free, but he held onto her, drawing her back the way they had come. "Go on about your own business, Dob Biggers!" she blazed. "What're you doing here, anyhow?"

"They let out school, and I was going home to tell my folks. Then I seen Miz Macabe at the landing. She said you must've gone busting off after Miz Cowan." He glared at her. "You go on down to the landing, hear me? I'll go fetch your ma!"

Suddenly Letty quit fighting, her mouth open wonderingly. "How about your own folks?" she asked.

"They'll look out for theirselves," Dob said bitterly. "They always have in the pinches."

"Where's Amy?"

Dob looked worried. "She started to the upper landing with some stuff for the store. We pulled straws to see who went. I wish it had been me." He straightened his shoulders, then said sternly, "Get going, Letty, before the boats all leave. If your ma's to be found, I'll find her. I promise you."

He meant it. Here was a Biggers who would give his life for them, not the other way around. Yet she had always known that. She said softly, "Dob, I just can't go off and leave her."

He glared at her in exasperation, then said gruffly, "Then I'll go with you. Come on."

Letty didn't protest, although it might mean his life as well as hers. They went on until they came to the road to the mountain. Some people coming toward them went hurrying past without speaking. Her mother wasn't one of them. There were no more in sight up the road. She and Dob could hear gunfire, then, as well as the cannon, down on their right toward the river.

And then something happened to tell them there was no turning back. New gunfire erupted behind them. They stopped with drained faces to listen. It wasn't some settler's jumpiness, the shooting was continuous. Some of the Indians had reached the landing.

"Some of 'em had time to get away, Letty," Dob said. His voice was scratchy. "Miz Macabe was at the landing when I seen her. She and the kids had a good chance to get in one of the boats."

"I shouldn't have left them," Letty whimpered.

Dob seemed of the same opinion, but not because he considered it a desertion of her sister and brothers. "Well, it's too late now," he said harshly. "I reckon we could do your ma no good, now, even if we could find her."

"Let's keep looking."

"Letty, I've got to think of you. I'm going to do it, and you can hate me all you want. Come on."

She didn't protest the way he expected her to. She knew he was right, that persisting in her search, with no escape for her mother to come of it, would endanger his life as much as hers. When he saw she wasn't going to fight, he let go of her arm. They soon found themselves far back from the river and hurrying west. Before long Letty realized that they were on the back part of Toby's claim. And then Dob steered them down toward the river.

Presently Letty saw why. Below them was a long backwater that ran like a finger behind a thin spit, the slack water parallel to the river. Dob turned them down toward this, and by then the shooting was faintly distant, sounding like the drip of rain from a roof.

They came to the end of the slough, and Dob stopped on the bank, a scowl on his face. "Well, they took it. There'd have been room for more, but did they think of anybody else? They took it and away they went."

"Took what?" Letty asked.

His eyes were streaked with anger deeper than she had ever seen in human eyes. "There was a raft here. Me and Amy built it out of drift logs to fool around on. I figured they'd use it, but I sure didn't think they'd gone already." His mouth twisted. "They heard shooting, and that was enough for my pa and brother." All at once he sat down on the sandy bank, swallowing hard.

Letty looked down at him with her fear given way to the pain in her heart. There had been no reason except pure cowardice for the Biggerses to get away that fast. The Indians hadn't been this far down the river. They wouldn't bother with cabins so isolated unless they made a clean sweep at the landing and had things their own way. That bunch couldn't have known that Dob was bringing her with him, hoping to save her life. But they must have known he would head for home, even that Amy might have turned back and tried to get home, too. Yet they hadn't waited, even, for their own flesh and blood.

Sitting on her heels, she looked into his face. "Dob, it's all right. I'm not afraid as long as I'm with you."

That did something for him. After a moment he got to his feet. "Might as well go on to the house, but I know they're gone, and I bet they both took their guns."

They went on. It was the first time Letty had ever been at the Biggers place, and she was shocked by its poverty and slovenliness. She waited outdoors while Dob went into the cabin. He came out in a moment shaking his head.

"No use looking at Toby's. They took both guns. Must've figured the redskins'd chase 'em all the way down to Portland."

For the first time Letty understood why her mother hated the older Biggerses like she did. How much worse it must be for Dob with them his closest kin, people he couldn't detest and ignore as her mother did. Dob was silent, and she knew he was putting something through his mind.

"Might as well stay here as long as they let us," he decided. "You can go in the house and rest if you like. I'll stay out and keep an eye peeled."

Letty knew he was trying to protect her life with his own, that if prowling stray Indians showed up he would try to lure them away from the cabin and her. She shook her head. "I won't go in unless you do."

He grinned, an expression not deep but a change from his hurt and anger. He said, "You've got plenty of sand in your craw, Letty. Come on. If we go up in the attic we'll be out of sight. And we could see better what's happening at the landing."

"All right."

She knew he was ashamed of the inside of the cabin. No wonder, for it was a disordered mess. The loft ladder went up from the kitchen, and Dob went straight ahead of her. She followed him into an attic divided in two by ragged blankets. She could tell from the attempts to decorate it that the half they came into was Amy's. The bed was by the window. Dob pulled the foot end away from the wall so they could sit on the side of it and see out. She sat down and looked.

She could see the landing's buildings, but as doll houses for they were so far up the river. A haze hung over them in the cold March light, maybe powder smoke, but only by listening carefully could she tell that there was still fighting there. She felt safer. As long as that continued, there wasn't much danger of Indians venturing down where they were.

She said wistfully, "I wonder if any boats got off."

"Hard telling," Dob admitted. He didn't want her thinking about that and changed the subject. "Letty, come night we got two choices. Take our chances and stay here. Or start walking down the river bank as far as we can get in the dark."

"Which do you want?" she asked.

"It's up to you."

"I think I'd rather stay here."

He sighed and nodded. "That's how I feel, too."

She knew he was thinking about Amy, the only one in his family he could possibly love. Just as she was thinking about her mother and Win and Matt. And maybe the younger ones, if Molly hadn't got them away in a boat. To leave seemed like deserting them all in order to save their own lives. That was the specialty of the older Big-gerses. Dob wanted no part of it, nor did she.

Something welled in her heart, and she said falteringly, "Dob, maybe we're going to die, so I want you to know this. I never counted you and Amy to be like—well, the others. Nor did Win and Matt and the youngsters."

"I already knew that," Dob said. "And if we get through this, Letty, I'm going to amount to something. So's Amy. We swore it together."

"You both amount to something," Letty said. "Already."

They stayed there unmolested through the long afternoon, for neither side at the embroiled landing seemed able to gain its way. Toward evening Dob went down to the kitchen and brought up cold biscuits and some water. Afterward Letty watched with dread the fading light. Dob judged that, from the stubborness of the defense, such people as remained at the landing had taken refuge on the wharf boat. A good barricade could be made by piling up freight, and there would be only one side from which the Indians could attack. But shortly after nightfall there was no mistaking that the fury of the fighting had increased.

"They've brought in more redskins," Dob decided. "They're pushing to get it wound up."

This was proved when in only a few minutes they saw the first fire. Dob didn't have to explain that part. Letty knew the Indians were burning the landing, which meant they were pretty much in control. A new fire appeared in the night, and then a lot of them all together. The sound of the shooting increased. She thought of the dogtrot, her mother's eating-house and the new house Matt had built. Yet this was nowhere near as important as the lives she was so worried about. Surely the Indians would overwhelm the defenders of the wharfboat at any minute. Before long the spot up there seemed to be all one fire.

Finally, Dob said, "Maybe we'd better not stay here any longer. They've sure got things going their way."

"Whatever you think."

She was glad to get out of the loft, for she had started to feel trapped. They went down the ladder and out into the yard. The air was cold, for the westerly wind had stiffened. She could see the sparks it was blowing from the fires. She followed Dob down into the brush by the river.

They had been there quite a while, Letty shivering and trying to keep her teeth from chattering, when something appeared on the river above. Dob sprang to his feet, staring. Finally, turning his head, he said, "They cut loose the wharf boat."

"The—Indians?" Letty faltered.

"No. The folks in it." Dob's voice was a mixture of admiration and worry. "That's pretty smart. Unless the siwashes can rustle boats to chase 'em, they can keep going till they reach Fort Vancouver."

Letty's first feeling was relief. Surely if Molly hadn't got the children into a boat earlier, she would have fled with them to the wharf boat. So now they would get away, no matter what terror they had undergone all day. And then she realized there would be nothing left now but Indians and maybe other stragglers like themselves trying to hide.

Dob thought of that, too. He said uneasily, "We've got to try and flag 'em down and go with them."

But, for safety's sake, the wharf boat had steered too far out on the river. They saw it come near, growing bigger than a steamboat. They could see men out on deck, clumsily steering with improvised sweeps. She and Dob risked the danger of Indians lurking near them and yelled and flailed their arms, trying to attract attention. Ponderously and unseeing, the odd craft slipped on down the river and disappeared into the night.

Chapter 15

The voice seemed faint and hollow, like somebody hollering through a pipe. "Letty—Letty—*look!* It's the *Belle!*"

Letty pushed at the layers of fatigue that covered her, reluctant to let go of a dream. It had taken her back to the house where they had lived when she was a little girl. It had been so hot in summer there that sometimes the family slept outdoors on the lawn. She had felt again the hard earth under her, the empty night about her and had seen the star-flung sky. And she had felt almost afraid but not quite. Her family had all been there, her father as gay and full of life as he had ever been.

Slowly she realized that the earth under her was really river sand. The blanket over her was a ragged quilt Dob had taken from the cabin before they slipped down the river and found a lonely place to hide for the night. She hadn't meant to go to sleep, only to keep warm under the blanket. Now it was broad daylight. She sat up groggily, and all at once her heart went wild.

Dob had gone down to the river shore and was dancing excitedly and waving his arms. On down the river the prow and house of the *Belle* broke the distance, just as she had seen it do uncounted times. There were dark-clad men all over her. Letty sprang to her feet, suddenly knowing what had Dob so excited. They were soldiers. She went racing down to him.

126

Dob had no time for her. He was too busy trying to attract the pilot's attention. That proved unnecessary. The *Belle* came on slowly, for those aboard knew what had happened. She was hunting a place to land. If she went on up where the Indians were, the soldiers would have to fight their way ashore. This was as good a place as any, and when they saw Dob, somebody put a glass on him to make sure he was friendly. Letty could see the glint of its lens. Then the *Belle* swung at a long angle, nosed to the flat shore and held herself there with her paddles. The passengers boiled off, armed to the teeth and looking angry. Some of them lifted a small cannon ashore.

The officer who directed everything came over to Letty and Dob. It pleased Letty when he touched his cap to her respectfully. "Lieutenant Sheridan, ma'am. Are there any more survivors near here?"

Letty shook her head, and Dob said, "It's not likely."

"Then you two get aboard. She's going back down the river. They're recruiting volunteers down there, and they'll need her for transportation up here." Letty started to object to leaving, now that help had arrived, with more coming. Sheridan seemed to read her mind, for he added gently, "It's best that you go, miss. We intend to make it hot here again. We'd as leave not have you to worry about."

He was right, and Letty let them lift her aboard the *Belle*. Dob followed. For them it was over, yet she was leaving too much of her heart behind to be glad. . . .

Lieutenant Phil Sheridan, who in a very few years was to distinguish himself as a commander of cavalry in the War Between the States, had been fully informed of the situation confronting him. Several boatloads of women and children had reached Fort Vancouver late the afternoon before. He could muster only forty dragoons, a weak force against the estimated number of hostiles. So he had rushed word to Portland, asking for civilian volunteers and commandeering the *Belle,* which by chance had laid over there that day to clean her boiler. By two o'clock in the morning the *Belle* had reached the fort, loaded, and was on her way upriver. En route they had met the wharf boat going down and held alongside long enough to obtain the latest information.

Sheridan knew he faced a grim situation, but he didn't know yet just how grim. His first objective was to lift the siege on the blockhouse at the middle rapids. Then he would go on to the upper landing, hoping that additional troops would have arrived by then from Fort Dalles. It was to take him over twenty-four hours even to reach the blockhouse.

His first step was to lead a patrol of six men on a reconnaissance, leaving the rest of the command where the steamer had deposited them. Everything along the way lay in ruins, and they saw dead cattle and horses, chickens, hogs, geese, all senselessly slaughtered by the savages. Quietly as the *Belle* had come in, her arrival seemed not to have escaped detection. The landing had been vacated by the hostiles and lay wholly devastated. Beyond, where the negotiable land narrowed to a neck, Sheridan ran into trouble so abruptly that a bullet grazed his nose and killed a soldier beside him. The Indians, and there were hordes of them, had drawn a line between his small force and the blockhouse that they meant to hold. A frontal assault would be suicidal. Until he had devised a strategy, Sheridan had to convince the Indians that an attack by them would be equally costly.

He did this by bringing up the rest of the command and the cannon. The Indians had grown somewhat used to the blockhouse howitzer, but they were sufficiently timid that the new one kept them under cover. Through the rest of the morning and a long afternoon neither side dared to advance. But a frontal attack was the least of Sheridan's intentions. His foragers had scared up a bateau somehow overlooked by the refugees and brought it to the ruins of the landing well downstream from the deadlocked battle.

Early the next morning Sheridan poured a few more cannon shots into the Indian line and then seemed to retreat. But at the landing he began to send his men across the river in the bateau, twenty at a time, hidden from the Indians above by Strawberry Island which, ages before, had caused the river to meander. The Oregon shore was precipitous, and once there Sheridan climbed high enough to see that the island was loaded with noncombatant Indians. They were so sure of victory they were passing the time running horse races and feasting on beef stolen from the settlers. His men could pick their way along the Oregon shore, but pulling a boat upstream from that bank was impossible. Sheridan and ten men crossed to the island. Under the noses of several hundred unsuspecting Indians of mixed sexes and ages, they towed the boat to the island's upper end.

In another hour he had outflanked the warriors holding the line on the narrow neck on the Washington side. The water above the island was calm and smooth, and two boat trips put the command across on the blockhouse side. They were seen from the blockhouse, which had grown aware of their arrival. But Kelly and his refugees refrained from cheering. They knew there were four times as many painted savages in the vicinity as there were bluecoats.

Sheridan wanted much more than to lift the siege. He hoped, once there were reinforcements, to deliver a reprimand that the Indians would never forget. He moved toward the blockhouse, meeting little resistance, and all at once halted in consternation and anger.

Just up the portage tracks a bugle rang out, the sound rattling off the rocks and shivering the air itself, telling every Indian in the vicinity what was up. A moment later Colonel Steptoe and a column of over a hundred regulars, brought down from the interior, stepped smartly into view. Steptoe was Sheridan's senior by a considerable margin. But when the two officers came together, Sheridan delivered himself of his opinion.

"Well, colonel, we'll bag a lot of guilty Indians after that announcement."

The senseless blast of the bugle, by which Steptoe had given some routine command, had lifted the siege at a cost of only a little air from the bugler's lungs. It was an invitation to the hardcore hostiles to slip away and live to fight another day. . . .

Amy knew she would never forget her feelings that morning when the *Mary* and *Wasco* drew in sight of the upper landing. The settlers in Bradford's store had waited through a night and a second day. The Indians had tried from daylight to dark to burn the store by throwing firebrands from the bluff top. During the night they had burned all the other buildings to light up the surroundings and prevent any attempt at escape. Even the hardiest of the defenders hadn't seen how they could get through yet another day. And then, before the day was very old, somebody had let out a tremendous yell.

"They're coming! The steamers're back!"

Men yanked the shutters off the riverside windows so everyone could see. Amy squeezed into a place just as the steamers' throaty whistles announced their impending arrival. Both vessels were so loaded with men and baggage they rode low in the water, and the *Wasco* towed a flatboat with horses for the dragoons. When the Indians on the bluff saw the same sight, the shooting died away. The firebrands stopped raining down from atop the bluff.

Colonel Wright, Amy soon learned, was making up for his neglect, for he had come in person, bringing two hundred soldiers. On the morning of the attack, he had moved out of Fort Dalles for the interior with all but a garrison force. So when the steamers reached Dalles City to get help, Wright had been going into camp at Five Mile Creek, a day's march distant. A courier from the garrison had reached him there. Then it had been necessary to march all the way back and load aboard the two steamers. With the boats so heavily loaded and a flatboat in tow, they had made slow progress. They had got only as far down as Wind Mountain on the second day of the siege. They had tied up at the bank there overnight.

But Wright had arrived at the upper landing early the next morning, and his whistle blasts had done what Steptoe's bugler did before him. They scared away every guilty Indian in the vicinity. . . .

Matt was better. All through another long day and night Libby had cared for him, bathing him in cold water and

keeping cold cloths on his forehead. At last his fever came
down, and he regained consciousness. When he could talk
a little, she was sure there had been no lung damage, so
there was hope. When he could eat some of the scarce
food in the cabin, he became a little stronger. Although
she persisted, she had a feeling that she was saving his
life only for him to lose it even more horribly. They were
so nearly out of ammunition that none of the men shot
unless a hostile actually tried to move in on them. The
only thing that kept the settlers alive that long was whatever had happened to draw off most of the savages.

And then, early on the last morning, Indians streamed
in from everywhere, and it seemed that the end had come.
But the warriors showed no interest in the cabin and only
went scurrying on into the deeper timber and away. Instead of more shooting, there was less and, finally, none
at all around the cabin.

"What in tunket brought that on?" George Fielding
wondered.

No one knew at the moment, but not long afterward
they all understood. A company of dragoons came riding
over the road from the upper landing, bristling with arms
and looking for Indians. Libby was too worn to feel much.
Win was unhurt, and she felt that Matt would pull through,
that his tough strength would save him. But she knew
nothing of what had happened to Letty and John and
Margaret and Pip. She wasn't much helped when the officer
with the dragoons advised them to stay where they were.
He said Matt's cabin was one of the very few left standing
from one end of The Cascades to the other. Nor were the
others jubilant, for each had somebody to wonder and
worry about.

But it was safe enough for the other refugees to disperse,
and that afternoon the *Fashion* came up with two companies of volunteers from Portland. The *Belle* returned
with another company of regulars and more volunteers
from Vancouver. Soon an armed force greater than The
Cascades had seen or dreamed of was scouring the area.
But the only Indians to be found were gathered on Strawberry Island. Although they claimed to have taken no

part in the uprising, nine of them were hanged because the barrels of their rifles showed they had been fired recently.

Locking the stable after the horse had been stolen, Colonel Wright told the settlers that two full companies of regulars would be stationed at The Cascades, one at each landing, with suitable blockhouses built for them. The portage trestles had been burned, with thousands of feet of the wooden track torn up and thrown on the fires. But it would be put back in service at the earliest possible date. It was all the more important, now, and it and the steamboats would be busier than ever.

None of this meant much to Libby until the *Belle* came up again bringing those who had escaped by water. For the first time Libby gave way to tears, for among these were her four younger children, unharmed and mighty glad to be home.

Only then could she bring herself to leave the wood ranch and visit the lower landing. What she saw there dried her tears and hardened the line of her jaw. She had heard, yet seeing it was like a blow in the stomach. She had brought Win with her, and together they looked at the smoldering ashes, charred timbers, twisted metals and scattered bricks where their dogtrot had been. All that remained of the house Matt had spent his savings and so much work on was a bigger heap of the same. The landing, the neighborhood cabins, remained only as similar piles of ruin. There wasn't an animal or a domestic fowl left alive.

Something in Libby's eyes made Win swallow and say, "Mamma, compared to some we got off easy."

"I know." There had been a mass funeral the day before. Eleven civilians and three soldiers had died. Fourteen others had been wounded, with two of these hurt beyond hope. "But your education?"

"It doesn't matter."

"Oh, but it does!" Libby felt something within her turn hard as rock. There had been relief in Win's eyes, a sudden, almost palpable easing. "It's delayed a while, but it will still come. You hear me?"

His countenance darkened. Then he nodded his head.

She had to do again what she had done after Alister was taken from her. But then she had been a little younger and much less tired. She poked around in the ruins, weighing and considering. Her business was gone. The portage was so badly damaged it would be out of operation for weeks, maybe months. Even the sawmill that turned out the timbers for it had been burned to the ground. There was no sign of her cows and chickens so she could not, as in the beginning, sell milk, butter and eggs.

She was reduced to nothing but land, courage, and the river that had done her as much harm as good. Except for the savings that were to have turned Win into a man of the law. Fortunately these had been in coin, buried inside the iron fence where Alister lay. She could use them to send Win away in the fall, as she had planned for so long. What then of Letty and the other three, who also must have a full schooling in their turns? Besides, she had to have a new building and equipment for her eating-house. They all must have a new place to live. Win had to wait until future savings had come, coin by hardearned coin.

That night at Matt's cabin Libby realized how utterly tired she was, with a fatigue not to be relieved by a night's sleep. The wood ranch would be their home a long while. There she must share Matt's bed, the cabin being so small and they so numerous, but in his condition that was of no consequence. Yet in the night she felt a compelling temptation to give up her struggle and become his full wife. She was young, and the body could want, even when the heart didn't love.

Matt was an enterprising man. While he had lost his woodyards and the money he had put into the new house, he would be back on his feet far sooner than she. She could use her savings to send Win away as planned. Away from the things that were taking him from her. Away from the pretty Amy and the riverboats that so attracted him. Matt would be more than willing to see that the other children followed in turn. She nearly reached out to touch Matt, to promise herself when he was well. The hand faltered and withdrew.

When she went down to the landing the next day she carried a shovel, and that time she went alone. She saw men working everywhere, clearing away the ruins. The sight made her pull back her own shoulders and lift her head. A kinship she had never felt before brightened her eyes. All of them had lost something to The Cascades now, the same as she, and in many cases it had included someone dearly loved. They were digging out to build again, as she must. They would build better, profiting from earlier mistakes. It was the river that made all that possible, and she shouldn't go on hating it.

She knew Alister's grave hadn't been harmed and she hadn't looked at it, but now she did. This time she unlocked the iron gate and went into the enclosed plot, which was large enough to receive them all in time. No one was near her, but for a long time she pulled wild grass and weeds and threw them over the fence. Then, checking once more to make certain she wasn't watched, she began to dig around the rose bushes. Under each one there was a glass jar or two, undisturbed. The money was all there. She sealed it away from covetous eyes again and finished spading the rose bed. Then she rested, sitting in the grass and thinking how nice it looked.

And then, because she never came there without trying to reach the man she loved, she grew quiet and thoughtful and then summoned him.

"Alister? We're still here, all of us. But you know that. And everything I pledged before, I pledge again. I can't be Matt's wife, no matter how he wants and deserves me. I can't let our children grow up any way but the one you wanted."

His response came in her heart, filling it. It came in her mind, setting it. It came in her body, extinguishing its disloyal desire for any other man. She picked up the shovel and went on to the landing to start clearing away the ruins.

Chapter 16

Matt was returning from his first wood haul to Dalles City for the year, in a balmy day of late March, when he saw the horse at the Wind River landing, and the figure beside it that was waving vigorously. He heard a chuckle at his elbow. It came from Danny Hughes, his deckhand on these runs and otherwise a yard hand at the upper Cascades woodyard.

"Don't laugh," Matt said. "You've got to get the horse aboard, as well as the pretty girl."

"If I balked, you'd do it," Danny said.

"Well, don't let her know it. She's spoiled enough, already."

"And who done it?" Danny retorted.

Matt frowned, for Danny knew it hadn't been her mother who had spoiled Letty. By then he was steering a course toward the landing that served the new settlers in the Wind River district. Moments later the bow touched lightly against the landing bumpers, and Danny leaped ashore with a line.

Matt waited at the wheel, thinking how like a boy Letty looked in a pair of Win's outgrown pants and one of his old shirts. A sweater finished the disguise of her chest and a scarf hid her pretty hair. She stood slack-postured and smiling up at him, while Matt stared sternly back at her. Officially, he was obliged to frown on these sallies of hers. Libby would take off his hide if she knew how far the girl

135

ventured away from home on the horse he had given her on her seventeenth birthday, a year before. He took his time before he started down to help Danny. They threw out the gangplank and watched Letty lead the horse aboard for the ten-mile ride on down to the upper Cascades.

Not fooled a bit by Matt's stony countenance, Letty said cheerily, "How did you happen to notice me from way out on the river?"

He wasn't going to admit he had been watching and hoping she would be there, as she had done often the summer before. "I'll ask the questions. What're you doing way off here by yourself? And don't you know it's a lot of trouble to make a landing just to take aboard you and that nag?"

Letty stroked the nose of the horse. "Hear what he called you, Percy?" She had named it Nez Percé Chief but hadn't left it long in that form. "The nice man who paid a hatful of money to buy you for me."

They tied the horse to the mast and pulled in the plank. Letty followed Matt to the wheelhouse while Danny cast off the lines. Secretly, Matt was pleased that Letty had as much enthusiasm for his old wood scow as Win had shown in his day. Once they were safely away from shore, he let her have the wheel without waiting for her to beg him. She grasped it eagerly, her eyes bright. She was a pretty thing, and he didn't really mind her knowing how completely he doted on her.

Loading his pipe, he said, "What're you supposed to be doing, instead of this?"

"Well, I had to come to the store for some things," Letty said. "Since I was so close, it seemed a pity not to ride on up and meet you."

"Which only delayed your getting home by three or four hours."

Letty tossed her head. "Oh, Mamma won't notice. She'll be too busy counting the money she made today."

"You oughtn't to say things like that."

"I know," Letty said contritely. "I guess it's because she gives me such a time."

Matt nodded. Libby would never understand that her

older daughter had every bit of her own spunk and set of mind. Letty had grounds for her dig about Libby's obsession with money. For most of the five years that had passed since the uprising, Libby had had a difficult time. In consequence, she had given the rest of them a hard time, too. Matt didn't like to think about that, when he had prospered handsomely.

The Indians had demonstrated at The Cascades that taming them wouldn't be the easy undertaking everyone, including the army, had expected. The job had taken not that one summer but over two years in which General Wool got so wrought up he closed the interior completely to settlers and miners. This had nearly spelled ruin for Libby, for while the portages hummed once more the traffic was even more military than before.

In trying to destroy The Cascades, the Indians had given the portage itself a better grip on life. Captain Baughman had replaced the *Mary* with the much larger *Hassaloe*. His competitors on the Oregon side countered with a stern-wheeler even larger, the *Idaho*. Joe Ruckel, who was part-owner of the *Fashion*, put in a wooden, mule-powered railroad on the Oregon side to replace the pack trains, and villages sprung up over there. The Bradfords responded by improving their track and incorporating as the Cascades Railroad. In return, Ruckel and his partner Olmstead named their six-mile line the Oregon Portage Railway.

It was partly in fun but mostly in dead earnest, for the men involved sensed big things to come for them all. And new men became interested, the foremost being Captain John Ainsworth, who previously had confined his interest to the Willamette and lower Columbia. Now he moved into the upper river, organizing most of the fleet into the Union Transportation Line. He put the big *Carrie Ladd* and *Mountain Buck* on the run to The Cascades to use the Bradford portage and connect with the new *Hassaloe*. The boats ran on alternate days so that The Cascades had daily service both up and down the river. It was, Matt thought, as if Ainsworth smelled what was waiting, right around the corner.

Libby never sensed the rainbow that was to follow the

troubled years she endured. With the fighting, and then with the interior cut off completely to civilians, there were never more than a few measly travelers to patronize the restored business that had taken her savings. It had made Matt feel downright mean that he, himself, was so lucky. With all the new traffic, and all the new boats, and with Dalles City booming as never before, his wood business had been back on its feet overnight. Now it was making him more money than he knew what to do with.

The rainbow had been a true one, with pots of gold on either end. The first glittering strikes, in quantities never dreamed of before, were on the Kamlops, the Fraser, and in the Cariboo deep in Canada. That had come two years ago, Matt reflected, and the next summer saw more fabulous strikes much nearer, first on the Clearwater and then on the Salmon. Word trickled in from the prospectors scattering everywhere that equally staggering finds were impending in the Boise basin, on the Powder, John Day and Owyhee. New towns sprang up everywhere, some at the diggings and others on the traffic routes, and behind the miners came the hordes who served or preyed on them. In each of the two years since the first finds, some ten thousand boat passengers had used the portages. The freight was in proportion, and the volume of both increased by leaps and bounds. . . .

Matt came out of his reverie to see the upper landing rise as from the water, far down ahead. Letty released the wheel to him, and then she was the one who stood thoughtfully watching through the windows. Both sides of the river had developed into neat little towns. Settlers were spreading out from the newer one on the Oregon side. The country was settling up, and there was no denying it.

He knew why the girl beside him had grown so soft-eyed. Soon after the uprising, Dob Biggers had gone to work on the old *Mary*. Now he was third officer on the new *Hassaloe*, which lay at the dock on the Washington side. At the end of a long struggle with Libby, Win was now using the education she had drilled into him. It was helping him to discharge the duties of purser on the same boat.

Glancing at Letty, Matt said, "Seen him yet?"

"For a little while." Letty knew which of the lads he meant and was silent a moment. Then she added, "Matt, can I stay with you tonight?"

Matt frowned. "I guess you've been rowing with your mother again."

"Well—yes."

"I won't have you punishing her by staying away all night."

"It's not to punish her. Besides, I left word with Margaret that I might stay at the wood ranch."

"Your mother still won't like it."

"Please?"

He said with a sigh, "I reckon you've already got it fixed for him to come to my place tonight, too."

"Yes."

"Well—all right."

She rose quickly on her toes and kissed his cheek. "Matt?"

"What else?"

"Win's coming along with Dob. I arranged with Amy to come up from Beacon Rock. It'll be a party, and I love you."

She waited for him and Danny to tie up, then took Percy ashore. The woodyard was twice the size it had been when the Indians burned it. Now there was a barn for the yard teams and a riding horse he had acquired for his own use, his business keeping him on the go so much.

Letty said, "Meet you at the store after you've saddled up?"

Matt nodded, and she sprang lightly into the saddle and went spurting away toward the town. While he saddled his less beautiful horse, Matt talked with Danny and Howie Fleeson, the other yard hand. Then he followed Letty to the store. She had already come out and was putting something into her saddlebags. She glanced at him with twinkling eyes.

"I bought some cream of tartar and vanilla," she said. "We're pulling taffy tonight."

"Me and my forty-year-old teeth," Matt said.

"I hope I look as good when I'm your age."

Matt smiled, thinking how wonderfully fresh and young and desirable she looked at the age she was now. Like the younger Libby, except taller and not so weighted down with care. Yet his feeling for Letty had none of the fire that had raged for Libby. A fire not gone out but banked, now that it had burned unfed for so long.

They started up Mill Creek and onto the mountain. Letty fell silent, and Matt kept thinking how bad it was that she and Win had to use his place, and secretly, to see the young people they were the most interested in. He knew this grieved Letty, for she was a good girl to the core and would never go wrong unless driven to it. But if driven too hard—well, he didn't let himself think about that.

They reached the cabin with the March day about gone. There was a fence around it now, and grass and flowers, and the cabin itself had been enlarged. Matt had done this, hoping it would help convert Libby's enforced stay there, after the landing was burned, to permanent residence. He knew her children still liked it better than the cramped box house she had built on the site of the old dogtrot. When she made the move back, he hadn't liked the idea but, knowing her changeless need for personal privacy, had given in.

They put their horses in the barn, took care of them, and then went to the cabin. Letty shoved him out of the kitchen, where he was as much at home as she, and made their supper. She was happy over the coming evening, and yet troubled. He guessed that the latest quarrel with Libby had been a bad one. He built a fire in the stone fireplace. There was no need to fix up the place for the party. He was by instinct a neat and orderly man.

They had eaten, and Letty had tidied up the kitchen before she opened up again. They were sitting by the fire, Matt sucking on his pipe. "Matt," she said hesitantly. "I know I can tell you this. Dob and I plan to get married in June."

"So that's it."

"Don't you be against it, too. I couldn't stand it if *you* objected."

"You know I'm not against it." He scowled at the fire. "Just against it having to be this way."

Old Mose had finally boozed himself to death. Sarah had followed within the month, as if she had nothing to live for without him there to rant at and slave for. Matt had hoped this would make a difference with Libby, but it had made none. Maybe this was because Toby was still around to keep the memory of her embittering experience fresh. More likely, it was because time had stood still for Libby ever since the day it stopped for Alister.

Matt could understand that. He had liked Alister Arlen. He had only to remember how Libby's eyes had warmed every time she looked at her husband to know how deeply she had loved him. Yet he had a feeling that, over the years, he had come to understand Alister's wishes for his children better than Libby had interpreted them. More and more he had championed them. Each time he had done so he had sacrificed a little more of his always slim chance of winning her heart, himself.

When two years had passed after the Indian attack without Libby's getting back on her feet, she had come to him. Humbled and despairing, she had asked for the loan of money to send Win off for his final schooling. Matt had refused her. And then he had told her what Win had never had the heart to reveal himself. That he hated the idea of becoming a lawyer and yearned to go on the riverboats as Dob had done already. And now, Matt thought, the screws were turning on him again over Letty.

He and Letty heard sounds they both waited for, that of horses coming from toward the upper landing. They stayed where they were and let Win and Dob come in to them. Matt felt something like a patriarch when he saw the two strapping young men. Both were in settler clothes but set proudly apart and—in their own minds a notch above —by their boat caps. Dob had eyes only for Letty, but Win came over to Matt, his handsome young face warmed by an easy grin. There had never been any gulf between them.

"Howdy, Matt." Together with Libby's yoke, Win had thrown off much that she had trained into him to distinguish and set him apart and had taken to using western language. Matt saw nothing wrong with that. From the start Libby's children had accepted their environment and, to the extent that she would allow, had adapted themselves to it. "I thought maybe you'd give us a race, today, when we passed you coming down."

"Cap Baughman's a friend of mine," Matt said. "I'd hate to shame him. If you want a race, why don't you take on the *Idaho?*"

"Cap's trying to," Win said. "So far she won't take bait." There was excitement in his eyes. A lot of talk was being made about the comparative merits of the new boats. It was easy to see that the *Idaho* was larger, but which was faster had yet to be proved. Win went over and kissed his sister, saying immediately, "It looks like Amy hasn't got here yet."

"As if that wasn't the first thing you saw," Letty returned, smiling at him. They were as close as Dob and Amy. "Why don't you go meet her?"

Win said with a laugh, "As if that wasn't what I had in mind."

He was gone like a shot.

Dob took his eyes off Letty, finally, and came over to Matt. He was twenty-two, and while his face was still boyish it had a set, a quality of integrity that could never have issued from Mose Biggers. There must have been something in Sarah's line that had cropped up again in Dob and Amy.

Dob said, "Matt, how's tricks?"

"No complaints," Matt said. "How's Win doing on the *Hassaloe?* He half the river man he thinks he is?"

"Cap Baughman likes him fine. But Win's itchy." Dob laughed from the vantage point of being two years older and three years longer on the river. "He can't wait to be a captain, himself."

"Don't you have the same itch?"

"I sure do."

"You'll both be, some day. I'd bet my bottom dollar on that."

Letty, a little jealous of their conversation, said impatiently, "Come out in the kitchen, Dob. We might as well start the taffy."

Matt chuckled and let himself be deserted. He sat by the fire and smoked his pipe, contented and yet unrestingly troubled. Win came back with Amy, who had surprised no one by turning into a truly beautiful woman. To look at her, you would never believe the way she had slaved on the Biggers claim, after the death of her parents had delivered her and given her a free hand. Amy and Win too, repaired to the kitchen, and still Matt didn't intrude himself. He could have gone off to bed without being much missed. Yet he had to be able to swear, if Libby found out about this and called him on the carpet, that they had been chaperoned thoroughly.

It was after Win, Dob and Amy had gone that Letty let Matt know the full extent of the coming crisis. She looked happy and sleepy while she sat by the fire with him a moment before going to bed. She seemed hesitant yet eager when she said, "Amy whispered me something before they left. Want to know what?"

"Sure," Matt said. He did and didn't, in fear it would add to his secret troubles.

Letty's smile deepened. "Win wants them to make it a double wedding."

Chapter 17

Libby was face to face with Toby Biggers before she saw him. The *Mountain Buck* lay at warfside, pouring more freight into the glutted facilities of the portage. A week before, she had sent down to Portland for materials to make white shirts for John, he now being the one she was preparing to send off to school in the fall. The package hadn't arrived, so she was already in an exasperated mood when she crossed back over the wharf to see Toby. He stood in a spot of April sun, taking his ease while he watched more industrious men unload the steamer and load the portage cars. But his eyes shifted to her, Libby saw, and there was a grin on his whiskery face.

Her step faltered, but she had to pass him to reach her place of business, so she went on in purposeful strides. In the ten years since they first reached The Cascades she had come close enough to him to speak no more than two or three times. Even so, he had given her that look of lecherous impudence each time, chuckling to himself as if the joke was on her when she cut him cold. In another ten years he would be the looking-glass reflection of his father.

When she came abreast of him, Toby touched his old black hat and said, "Howdy, Miz Cowan," and laid flat, brazen eyes on her face. When she failed to return the greeting, he moved slightly to block her way. "Why, Miz

144

Cowan. You ought to at least give me a how to do. We'll be all one family pretty soon."

Libby stopped dead in her tracks, looking into his amused eyes.

"What are you talking about?"

"Why, our young 'uns," Toby said with relish. "The double hitch they figure on."

"I have no idea what you're talking about." Libby tossed her head, but she was sick to her stomach.

"Why, it looks like they ain't told you." He grinned jeeringly. "My, I hope I ain't let the cat out of the bag. I figured they'd told you like they done me, with their pas both dead, and us being sort of the heads of the families."

Tears blinding her eyes, Libby cut past him and ran on to the eating-house. The day's work was over, and she had been on her way home, but now she unlocked the door and slipped inside, needing to compose herself before she went home and faced Letty. For once she failed to be uplifted by the new quarters for her business, which had corrected the mistakes in the first building. She looked with blind eyes at the neat tables and clean, curtained windows, the papered walls, the well-swept floor, then went over and sat down on one of the benches.

Win she had given up as lost to her. And what a way to learn that none of her pleas and arguments and outright threats had had any effect on Letty. There had been hope, until now, that something would open the girl's eyes to the beauty, refinement and education she would throw away if she tied herself up for life with Dob Biggers. That was an honest and valid point, leaving Dob's background out of it.

Her mind went back to the humiliating day when she had been driven to ask Matt to loan her money to finish Win's law education. She had had no expectation that he would turn her down flatly. And then go on to tell her she was trying to pound Win into a mold he would never fit. And how the boy was going along with her plans only out of his feeling for her as his mother. That had ended the small chance there had been of Matt and herself ever truly uniting. Matt had known and accepted it for what he had called the sake of the children. As if he had a father's right, when she had supported them and repaid him for the first year when she had had to lean on him financially.

Having lost Win to Matt and the river, she had resigned herself as best she could to his eventual marriage to Amy. But Amy would become Amy Arlen. Letty, if she persisted in her insanity, would become Letty *Biggers*. The thought put a gagging feeling in Libby's throat. Never. She had made the only concession possible in giving in when the girl refused to be sent down to Portland to top off her education. She had known what a mistake that was, and now the mistake was back to haunt her.

Absolutely not. If Win wanted to finish throwing away his life, let him marry his Amy. But she would find a way to save Letty from such folly. She would see to it that the other children weren't exposed to the temptations that had brought on this situation.

Ready to face her older daughter, Libby stepped outside and locked the door. A quick glance showed her that Toby was still on the wharf, a slack, shiftless figure in a scene of decent industry. Again the taste of acid filled her throat. She walked quickly on along the path toward the plain box house that had replaced the dogtrot. She looked briefly, as she came near, at the site of the fine big house Matt had built for them only to have it burned to the ground before it was ever lived in. The charred debris had been hauled away, wind and rain had scoured the ground clean, and now grass had reestablished itself there.

The same thing must have happened to the place in Matt's heart she once had occupied, she thought. His gift of charity had all shifted from her, and a large share of the children's affection had been turned to him, as well. Once it had been Win, and now it was Letty who spent every minute possible with him. He probably had heard about the wedding plans, while she had had to be informed by Toby Biggers.

Letty was often off on the horse Matt had given her, but she was home when Libby went on and entered the house, sitting by the heating stove in the cramped living room. She was embroidering pillowcases, a thing all girls did for their hope chests and which Libby had encouraged until she learned the direction of Letty's mind. The boys were off outside somewhere. Margaret wasn't in evidence, either.

Letty went on with her needlework, saying casually, "Hello there."

Libby skinned off her overshoes and hung up her coat. "Where is everybody?"

"The boys said they were going up on the slough to look at their trap line. Maggie wanted to go over to see Patience Early. I told her she could."

"Don't call her Maggie," Libby said.

"Why not? All her friends do."

"Margaret's a pretty name, and Maggie's so ordinary."

"What's wrong with being ordinary?" Letty looked up then. Her eyes were truly wonderful, while Margaret squinted. Oh, this one was her beauty, her real secret love, her hope for herself reincarnate. "I mean," Letty amended, "being like the others here?"

Irritated, Libby said, "Like Toby and Stella Biggers?"

Letty looked surprised. "Who mentioned them?"

"I did." Libby knew she was handling it all wrong, but she couldn't hold back the anger that had boiled up in her. "I just talked to Toby for the first time in years. A real interesting conversation. He told me about the double hitch that is evidently planned."

Letty put down her embroidery hoop, cautious and withdrawn. After a long minute, she said, "I was afraid of that."

"Nice hearing it from *him*."

"Yes," Letty agreed. "I'm sorry you did. He wasn't told anymore than you've been told. Not deliberately. He just worked it out of Amy and Dob in that sly way of his."

"Sly way? At least we see alike on your future brother-in-law."

Letty pinched her lips and was quiet through several breaths. Then she said calmly, "I don't like Toby, and I don't like Stella, but they're involved. Dob and Amy can't change that. Amy told me what happened. The three of them fell heir to Mose's claim. She and Dob wanted to buy

Toby's share and divide the land between the two of them. Amy's worked awfully hard on that claim since her parents died. Dob's helped all he can. You wouldn't know it. Fixed up, neat and clean, and Amy's done the work of a man trying to make it a paying proposition. Instead of selling, Toby had the gall to demand part of the income or else rent on his share of the land."

"Naturally. But why did she do all that if she intends to marry Win?"

"They want to live there. Win intends to stay on the river, but they'll need a home."

"To raise more Biggerses in. You said she'd intended to divide the old folks' claim with Dob. What does he want with it?"

Letty looked up at her. "To build a house on for us."

"How cozy. Win and Amy, you and Dob, Toby and Stella. Spending the rest of your lives side by side. No wonder he said we'd all be one big family pretty soon."

"I'm sorry he did that to you. I was afraid he would, but I didn't know how to stop him. He wanted to know why the claim had to be divided, why they wanted him out. They had to tell him enough that he caught on. He knew how you abominate them, how it would make you feel. I'm sorry. Matt's the only one any of us has actually told."

"Oh, I knew he'd be in on it. After encouraging it all along."

"He didn't encourage it," Letty said sharply. "Anymore than he encouraged Win to go on the river. He argued your way, but we always knew his heart wasn't behind what he said. He's a fine man. You should have married him."

"I did."

Letty pinched her lips into a wry smile. She shook her head. "I'm not a child anymore."

The attack wrested from her, Libby said in confusion, "You can't possibly understand that."

"Why not? I love a man with everything you could have felt for Alister Arlen."

"Why," Libby gasped, "you speak of him as a stranger."

"He would be. If he were alive to walk in that door, I

wouldn't know him. Maybe you wouldn't. He'd have
changed. You're the only one who hasn't."

"You don't know what love is."

"What do you think's made me defy you and hope
against hope I could win you around because I love
you, too?"

Bewildered and knowing she had lost more ground than
she had gained, Libby said weakly, "A lot you care for
me."

"If I didn't, I'd have run off and married Dob by now.
I've waited for a chance when we could really talk. I
thought for a minute this might be it. Then I'd have
told you what we hope for in June. Because there'd be no
wedding, with fuss and feathers, unless you approve. We'll
just quietly be married somewhere. So will Win and Amy.
Because you can't stop that part. One way or another,
June it will be."

So the daughter was lost, the same as the son had been
lost to her and Alister. Libby rose wearily and went into
her bedroom, the only one downstairs. Moving to the window, she stood looking down toward the river. How she
hated it for what it had taken from her. As soon as she had
accumulated enough money, she would leave The Cascades and go east, taking Alister and the other children
with her. John would go in the fall, but she and the others
would follow as soon as she could manage.

Letty made supper and cleaned up the kitchen afterward.
But the minute she was through she went upstairs to the
bedroom she shared with Margaret. Libby set the others to
their studies, trying to shrink her heart until it had room
only for the ones bent over their books, still obedient and
malleable. When John was the only one who hadn't
finished and been sent to bed, she closed the book he was
studying. Lifting her hand, she moved it fondly over his
dark hair.

"You want to do it, don't you, John?" she asked ten-
derly. "I mean go away next fall and learn the law and
have a practice like your father would have had?"

He looked surprised. "Sure I do. Why?"

"Well, you're not hiding something, are you? I mean something you'd rather do?"

"No. I want to do it, if you want me to. Really."

"Good. You were only six when Papa died. Do you remember him at all?"

"I guess not very well. It's been a long time."

"For you, yes. I suppose Margaret and Pip don't remember him at all."

"I don't think so."

"Do they ever talk about what they want to do when they're grown up? I mean—the way kids do when their parents aren't listening?"

"Well, Pip wants to go on the boats like Win." John grinned. "Maggie—I mean Margaret—says she just wants to get married and have babies."

That settled it for Libby. Of John she could be sure. But the other two had to be taken away before The Cascades had claimed them.

She wasn't happy but she felt settled and relieved not to have to fight what had been inevitable much longer than she had realized. The next day helped her, not only because it was busy and profitable but because it brought the first real feel of spring. The forests on the mountain slopes were brighter overnight. The new leaves on the lowland trees and brush had sprung into a new and vibrant life.

It seemed that the harder the winter the more abundant the spring. And the winter just passed had been the worst in her ten years at The Cascades. There hadn't been as much ice, that time, but much more snow. This had been especially true in the interior, where livestock had suffered terribly and died off in droves. The new mining camps on up in the mountains had been cut off for weeks, with food short and the trails closed. Great packs of snow lay up there to seed the streams and, in the end, the Columbia through the coming summer. And now this bursting out again of spring.

Chapter 18

Letty looked at Matt with tear-brightened eyes. "Can't you do something?" she asked.

"God A'mighty, girl." He would gladly move heaven and earth for her, but all he could do was lift helpless hands. She had been waiting in the cabin when he reached it, after a day at the cutting, and she had had his supper ready. Now they sat in the warm May evening on the front step. She had just told him she was sure her mother was preparing quietly to leave the West entirely pretty soon. "If your mother's set her mind to that, you, me and all the mules in Missouri couldn't stop her."

Letty said dismally, "And you're not stretching it a bit."

Matt struck a match and held it to his pipe. The May days were long, but this one was fading, and he was uneasy about her riding back to the lower landing in the dark. "Now, you better get on that nag and skedaddle, or I'll have to ride home with you."

"I planned it so you would." Letty smiled at him tremulously. "Because I want you to see and talk to her."

"What can I say?"

"Do you want her to leave us? With Pip and John and Maggie? Do you want *them* forced into the patterns she's picked out for them?"

"No, I don't."

"Then do something. Please?"

Matt clenched his fists. Here was another beautiful young

151

woman turning to him in her despair. Yet it was different with Letty. He knew she loved him and looked on him as a father more than she looked on the man whose specter had so haunted their lives. He could endure Libby's leaving The Cascades, just as he had stood so much else. But it would be a lifelong heartache to Letty and Win that their marriages had driven her away. He wondered if Libby could be planting hints of that in an effort to forestall the marriages. When it came to her hatred of the Biggers family, she would be capable of it.

He said gently, "You get home before it's too dark. I don't want to see her tonight. I'll think on it, and if I see light maybe I'll ride down and see her tomorrow."

It was like holding Libby would be, when Letty flung herself into his arms, crying against his chest, then lifting a tear-stained face to be kissed. He was trembling when he went with her to get her horse. He stood looking down the road until she had disappeared.

He was on the same road the next morning by eight o'clock, riding down toward the lower landing. The day promised to be another warm one in a series unprecedented for that time of year. At the first break in the timber he reined in to look down at the river, far ahead and below him. The spring freshets usually came in late May and early June, carrying off the snow melt from scores of distant mountains. This was the earliest he had ever seen the river run so high, and it was nowhere near its crest. The warm weather was doing it. If it continued, or they got warm rain up at the headwaters, the lower river would be all over the place.

The main road went down to the landing, but Matt turned and rode on along the branch that headed down to Beacon Rock. Presently he was on Toby Biggers' claim, and again he turned, following wheel ruts that meandered down to where Toby's cabin stood bare and unadorned. A dog wandered out to meet him, but it was too shiftless to bark. Stella Biggers came to the cabin door.

Her corn-colored hair hung about a moonlike face. Her fat body stretched the calico bag she wore, and her bare feet were in Indian moccasins. She had a look of simple-minded wariness on her face, for it was the first time he had ever been there. Matt stopped in the littered yard but kept saddle. It seemed strange, even to a man of his tolerance, to touch his hat to such a slattern. He could stand it, he thought. This was something Dob and Amy had to swallow every day of their lives.

He said, "Morning, Miz Biggers. Toby around anywhere?"

"Barn," Stella said.

Matt rode over and swung down at the barn door. Toby must have heard the voices, for he appeared in the doorway. He didn't speak. His shoulders had pulled up, his face was set, and his eyes were even more uneasy than Stella's had been. Matt understood it. Every time their lives had touched in the past, Toby had shown his skunk blood. It was plain to see that he remembered it.

Yet Matt said disarmingly, "Howdy, Toby. Pretty nice weather we're having."

Toby nodded and waited. When Matt didn't say anything more, he shifted his tobacco in his mouth. "Reckon we were due for some," he offered. "After that stinking winter."

"It was pretty mean," Matt agreed. He had expected Toby to find more to complain about than to be glad of. Ne'er-do-wells always did. "That's the trouble with this country. Rain, snow and ice a good half of the year. Sometimes I wish I'd headed to California instead of coming here."

Toby said with sudden interest, "You and me, both. Man, they say the sun always shines down there."

Matt nodded. "Living's pretty soft, from what I hear." He had a feeling he could put it over. The grass on the other side of the fence always looked greener to a fellow like Toby. "You ever think of selling out and going there?"

"I've thought of it. But who to? Everybody around here lives off the river, one way or the other. There's no call for farmland in a mountain gut like this."

"I reckon that'd depend on your asking price."

Toby was catching on to the fact that this was no idle

conversation. A crafty look spread over his face, and he said cautiously, "What would you say it's worth?"

"Well—" Matt mused a moment. "For unimproved land around here, five an acre would be a pretty good price."

"Who'd pay it?" Toby already knew, and slyness oiled his voice.

"I would. Sort of thought I'd like to join your piece onto mine."

Toby was interested but he shook his head. "You won't at five an acre."

"Then what would it cost me?"

"Plenty. Because you're trying to get shed of me before that wedding." Toby grinned. "You figure that'd make Miz Cowan more agreeable to it."

"It might," Matt admitted. "On the other hand, you'd like California better than here. I'll go ten an acre, you throw in your stock and buildings. Not that they're worth much. I'd take that off your hands to make it easier for you. Then you could take your stuff down on a flatboat to the Willamette, and there's a good wagon road from there on south."

It appealed powerfully to the avarice in Toby, but he said weakly, "You'll have to do better'n that."

"How much better?"

"You brought the deal to me, Cowan. So you do the talking."

"All right, I will. For more. Five thousand for your claim, your interest in the old folks's, and your agreement to get yourself to California as fast as you can travel."

Toby's eyes bugged. He knew the property involved wasn't worth a third of that, that the rest was what Matt thought it worth to get him out of the country. He wasn't satisfied that he had got that hiked to the limit and said craftily, "Double it, and you might get a horse trade."

"Huh-uh." Matt shook his head. "You don't like it here, Toby. I can make you like it a lot less. If you're fool enough to turn down more money than you could rake together the rest of your life, I'll see you do."

He turned and mounted. Stella was still outdoors and had moved nearer. He knew from the expression on her face that she had listened in on everything. Her excitement didn't exceed Toby's; he just hid his better. Yet Toby let him ride about a hundred yards before he yelled.

"Hey—wait—I'll take her for cash on the barrel head!"

Matt rode back, not to dicker anymore but to dictate, for Stella was grinning happily, and Toby looked only a little less pleased with the deal.

"I'll give you a thousand earnest money when you've got your stuff on a flatboat and ready to go," Matt said curtly. "I'll meet you in Portland to have a proper deal worked out on paper. You'll get the rest of the money when I see for sure you're on the road." He stared at Toby through a long minute. "There's one other thing. If you ever show yourself around here again, I'll give you the whipping I've owed you for ten years. You hear?"

Toby bristled, wilted and nodded his head.

Matt rode on to the other Biggers place, where Amy now lived alone except for the short periods when Dob could be there with her. Spring wheat was sprouting on the flat below the cabin, and Amy had broken ground for a big vegetable garden. The barn was in good repair now. The cows she had turned out to pasture, that morning, were of good blood. She had put up a chicken house, and its fence was taut, with the house itself whitewashed. The cabin had undergone a miracle. Gay curtains hung at clean windows. Wild shrubbery had been brought from the woods and planted along the foundations. Busy as Amy was, summer would see, there, an extravagance of flowers.

The dress Amy wore, when she came out to greet him, was gingham, neat, fresh and fitted skillfully to her shapely body, but it wasn't what she wore when she did the heavy, dirty work around the place. So he knew she was taking butter and eggs to the store at the upper landing, timing it so she would see Win when the *Hassaloe* got in from Dalles City.

"Don't glare at me like that," he teased, not swinging down. "I won't keep you long from being on your way."

She had really given him a smile that, like Letty's, always lifted his heart. "You know you can have my time anytime, Matt," she said with a laugh. "I'm just surprised to see you here."

"And you might not like the reason," he said, his face sobering. "I just made a deal with Toby. Him and Stella want to try California, it appears."

She blinked. "Deal? For land?"

"Not much else he's got anybody would want, is there?"

"No, but—"

"I'm buying him out," Matt said. "His claim and his interest in this one here."

"Why, Matt! Dob and I tried and he wouldn't listen. I mean his share in this one."

"He listened to me," Matt said. "You might think it was high-handed of me. If so, I don't blame you. It *was*. And I figured I'd better 'fess up before you hear it from him."

"I know what you really paid him for," Amy said, shaking her head. "And that he made you pay through the nose. Oh, Matt. I don't consider it high-handed. I'll be glad to be rid of him. Dob will be. But you were really thinking of—your wife, weren't you?"

"Sort of," Matt admitted. "Toby wasn't helping things there, either."

"I'm afraid his leaving won't help things there."

"I aim to have a talk with her."

"I wish you luck," Amy said wistfully. "From my heart."

Matt cut wide of Toby's cabin when he rode back toward the lower landing. With each step of the horse he grew more convinced that Amy was right and more angry with Libby because of that. When he stopped at the box house he winced, as he did each time he rode up to it. Cramped, ugly and flimsy, it was a mockery of the house he had built. It was also a monument, he reflected, to her sacrifice of everything to her obsessions. He caught her before she had left for the day's work, surprising and worrying her.

The young ones were pleased to see him, as they always were, but his face told them this was no ordinary visit. The gleam of hope in Letty's eyes troubled him, for all at once he had no hope left, himself. He had never felt it his place to order them around, but he said flatly, "You boys go clean the barn or something. And you better take off that coat, Libby. I want to talk to you."

"I haven't time," Libby retorted.

"Letty and Margaret can go down and help Molly till you get there."

"You bet," Letty said. "Come on, Maggie."

Libby looked defiant, then uncertain, and at last she shrugged and took off her coat.

Matt waited until he was alone with her. He didn't lift his voice, but it filled the room when he said, "When I leave here, you're going to hate me, Libby Arlen. Because I'm going to strip you naked. Not so I can see you. But in hopes you can be made to take a good look at yourself." She gasped, but he gave her no chance to interrupt. "As late as this morning I was fool enough to think that getting rid of Toby Biggers would ease your mind. Enough you'd let those young people get married without making them feel guilty, now and for as long as they live. So I bought Toby out. He'll be gone for good in another week."

"You—bought out Toby?"

"Lock, stock and barrel." Matt grimaced. "Five thousand dollars down the drain. About what I put into that damfool house."

Libby looked stunned. "Damfool house? And you called me Libby Arlen. Matt, what's come over you?"

"The truth. It was too simple to see till these marriages come up. You can't stop them, but you sure aim to spoil them if you can. Hush, now, and listen. The truth's not in you hating the Biggers family, including two innocents. It's not even in you trying to bring Alister and you alive again through at least one of your children. That's what you tell yourself, but it's wrong."

"Then what is the truth?" Libby said bitterly.

"You can't take a licking. Once you set your mind to something you just don't ever give up. And you'll keep taking lickings till you've been humbled and brought to terms with life."

Chapter 19

By late May the river ran higher than even the oldest Indians could remember seeing it. The rapids were all but smoothed out. The islands had grown smaller. Along the flatlands, sloughs and veritable lakes appeared that had never been there before. The wharfboat, which rose and fell with the stage of the river, was almost on a level with the eating-house.

Libby was aware of this and knew how everyone worried over the crest still to come in June, yet she found it a matter of indifference to herself. May's end and June's coming meant one thing to her, the marriages that were never mentioned in her presence, for which no formal wedding plans were being made, but which would occur, as Letty had threatened, just the same. Only because of this did she meet with dread and apprehension each new day.

She had never recovered from the morning Matt turned on her, so unexpectedly and so completely. Through a decade, her one abiding comfort had been the stone pillar he made for her life, and now it was gone. He couldn't have told her a thing about her default when it came to him. She had been conscious of it all the while. She simply could not accept what he had said, not on his own behalf but for the children.

It wasn't selfish mule-headedness to rise from defeat undefeated, as she had done twice in her life. It wasn't enshrining the memory of a loved one long dead to redeem the pledges she had made when he died. Without that direction and dedication, she couldn't have gone on. She had thought Matt understood, and it had been a knife in the heart to hear him talk as though he had awakened from folly, at last. She could only relieve the pain of it by reminding herself that he was wrong.

For one thing, she was far from the defeat Matt had said must come to humble her. As the season came on, and in spite of the high water, traffic on the portage reached unprecedented volumes. She and Molly filled their tables each day of the working week and often had to set second tables. There was no doubt that autumn would see her dream, now affixed to John, fulfilled. Resolved to sell the business before the slack season came in early winter, she had already begun to make preparations. From this Letty had guessed her intentions and had told Matt and probably Win. Libby hadn't minded, for there had been a chance that this would have some effect on the youngsters. It had had none at all, and they would soon know that it was no bluff.

When June arrived with a change of weather that broke the long warm spell, Libby still saw no cause for alarm. In spite of the high river stage, rainfall had been below normal. It was only catching up with itself in a massive spring storm. If things flooded, they would dry out again, and what was so bad about that? The steamers still arrived and departed, the freight still rammed through, and passengers still came to her tables hungry and left filled and pleased. What she failed to consider was that the drenching warm rains moved inland, just as the travelers did. Soon they were pouring on the massive snowpacks left by the winter at the headwaters, releasing a thousand times the water they brought down from the skies.

The first of it reached The Cascades in the dead of night. Libby, sleeping in her downstairs bedroom, was unaware of it until Letty, more wakeful upstairs, rushed down to arouse and tell her.

"I think they're piling sandbags at the landing, Mamma! There are all kinds of lanterns and men!"

As electrified now as she had been indifferent before, Libby scrambled out of bed. Shivering at the window, she saw the moving lights, softened into streaks by the curtains of rain. All she could understand was that some change had come, against which the portage and wharfboat crews were taking steps. Yet it frightened her. Her whole hope of the future was still centered there within a skip and a jump of the Bradford installations. If one was endangered, so would the other be. Turning hastily, she groped for a match and lighted a lamp.

Guessing her intention, Letty said quickly, "Don't go down there! What could you do?"

"Just you stay with the others," Libby told her. "And don't go waking them up. No use getting everybody excited."

"I'm going with you."

"No."

"Then I'll call John, and he can."

Libby considered. If there was danger of her building flooding, she would have to take steps, herself, and would need help. "Well—all right."

She dressed hurriedly. By the time she came out to the sitting room, Letty had lighted a lantern and laid out rain things for her and John. In a moment John came down the stairs, fully awakened by the emergency. Margaret and Pip followed, but Libby refrained from scolding and sending them back to bed. She saw by the clock that it was nearly three in the morning. She put on her boots and raincoat and hat while John did the same.

"I still don't know what you think you can do about it," Letty said worriedly. "That river's too much even for you."

Libby glanced at her in annoyance but said nothing. With a nod to John, she stepped out into the night and driving rain. Water ran along the footpath into a new brook. The mud was slippery, and the lantern John carried illuminated only a few steps at a time. Brush soon cut them from sight of the landing, but presently they could hear the wind-torn voices of men calling back and forth. Then, to her astonishment, they were confronted by a pond that lay squarely across their way.

"Gee whillikers!" John gasped. "The river's spilled over into the hollow somewhere!"

"I think we can wade it," Libby said, sounding calmer than she felt.

They made it across, although the water was nearly at boot-top depth. Here and there she could see a cabin's faint light. Her sense of urgency grew stronger. Then they came onto open ground and hurried on toward the landing. At first it made no sense, for there was only the light of lanterns set on perches or moving about. Soon she saw that Letty's guess had been right. They were building a dike out of sandbags between the wharf boat and port-age tracks. The wharf boat loomed higher than she had ever seen it and rose uneasily on its lines. Lights on the far shore indicated a like activity over there.

She and John moved closer, using their own lantern to see what was happening on the river side of the sandbags. What she saw nearly buckled her knees. Water already lapped against the bottom layer of sand-filled bags. Then a figure loomed beside them. Libby turned her head to see Harley Digby, who worked on the portage train. Rain streamed from his hat and made light-brightened beads on his beard.

She said in a voice made small by wind and concern, "What made it so much worse all at once?"

"Flooding in the interior," Digby said. "Word come down on the boats. Wallula's washed out. Dalles City's catching hell. And it's worse at the upper landing than here. With the river so wide, the narrows acts like a dam."

"Well," Libby said, "the narrows are good for something, at least."

"Not for long, Miz Cowan. Every drop of that water's got to come down past here."

Of course that was true, and she had only grasped at a straw. "Will the dike hold it away from the tracks?"

"Depends on how high and strong we can build it. We've got sand till hell wouldn't hold it, but bags are getting scarce."

Digby rushed on about his work. John said dismally, "The wharf boat looks like it might break loose any minute." Libby didn't care about that. The men didn't seem worried about it yet, either. They were working to save the portage track, and only as long as they could keep the water from it was her own building safe. She beckoned John, recrossed the tracks, and went over and unlocked her door.

"Light the lamps, John," she said. "I'll build a fire. We can have a place for them to get warm. Yes, and food and coffee, too."

"It's no place for you to be," John protested. "Letty was right about that."

Unhearing, Libby said, "I wish we could build another dike around the building. But that's out of the question. Where would we get sacks?"

Her rooms soon blazed with light, and there were fires in both stoves. She filled the big pot, ground a generous portion of coffee beans, and set the pot on the kitchen range to boil. She made extravagant inroads in her bread, butter, meat, bacon and eggs to prepare platters of sandwiches. Then she sent John out to pass the word that she was prepared and the workmen were welcome. They responded promptly, coming singly or in small groups to wolf a sandwich and drain down coffee, never staying longer than need be before rushing back to their work. She didn't mind that they tramped in mud and dripped pools of water on her clean floor. For the first time since she had lived at the landing she felt herself a part of it, generous and neighborly. And all the while she knew that this feeling sprang from her terrible need of them, her determination to keep them working to save the landing and her future.

She was so busy she was surprised to realize that it was growing light outdoors. She had heard enough by then to know that they had run out of bags to fill with sand and had resorted to hauling and piling rocks on the shore side to buttress and heighten the dike. She went to a front window and looked out to see with a spurt of hope that the rain had slacked to a drizzle. The dike looked like an impregnable barrier between her and the river. She couldn't see the wharf boat now but knew it had been eased down-stream to keep it from battering down the dike.

The men worked with less urgency, and the feeling grew in her that they had thwarted the rage and might of the river. Turning with a smile, she said, "You'd best go home now, John. Letty and the young ones must wonder about us."

"You better come, too," John said. "All they can do now is watch the dike and patch weak places. They can go home to eat. Some of them had gone already."

"I'll stay," Libby said.

"But if it gives way—"

"It won't give way," Libby snapped. "And you go on. You hear?"

John put on his raincoat and hat and, with open reluctance, left for home. Libby sat down tiredly, smiling at her ruined floor. She drank a cup of coffee but was too worn out to eat one of the leftover sandwiches. And too restless to sit still, she discovered. John had been right about the men having no further need of her, now that they were less pressed for time. She got mop and pail and carefully cleaned the tracked floor. She washed the stacked cups, the platters.

When she had finished, the clock told her it wasn't yet quite six. She should be sleepy but wasn't because, in spite of her self-reassurances, she was wound up tight. When she glanced out the window, she saw it no longer rained at all. That was a good sign. She steeled herself to go out-doors and take a better look at things.

The air outside her door carried a smell of spring again. The sky to the west was clearing fast, with a promise that the sun would break through before many hours had passed. She hurried across the portage tracks and climbed the rocks piled on the near side of the sand-bags. When she could see over, her heart nearly jumped out of her chest.

Angry brown water swirled and tumbled nearly to the top of the dike. It stood so high to Oregon that the far shoreline seemed completely strange. The islands had shrunk to a fraction of their original size. The lower rapids, up by Gant Island, had been smoothed completely flat. There was burden on the water itself, trees, sawed timbers, lumber, capsized skiffs. She turned so she could look west, and again she gasped. Down where the nearest slough hooked inland and back behind the landing and settlement, there was a broad expanse of angry water. She remembered the pond she and John had had to wade, and fear knifed into her heart. The water could creep a-round and behind the dike nullifying it completely. It endangered not only the landing facilities but the homes, including her own.

Her chest tightened when a man's voice spoke behind her. "You hadn't ought to be up there, Miz Cowan. You hadn't ought to be here at all."

She looked down at the concerned face of Linus Biddle, one of her companions during the Indian uprising. He was wet, muddy and looked bone-tired. She said falter-ingly, "How much higher do you think it will get?"

"God knows." He seemed resigned and concerned only for her. "We thought you'd gone. Come daylight, and we seen the backwater behind the settlement, we knew we had to evacuate the families. That's what they're all doing, now, and what you should be doing, yourself. The way she's rising, this thing'll go out in another couple of hours."

"Oh, no!"

She had all she could do to hide a whimper. If she yielded her business to the river, it would have brought her again to ruin. Letty and John were old enough to take care of themselves, Margaret and Pip. Biddle gave her a look of puzzled resignation and went on up the dike. Libby climbed down from the rocks and found a momentary relief in having the awesome scene cut off.

It came to her that she might save her equipment and supplies and be not quite so badly hurt if she lost the build-ing. Regretting that she had sent John home, she let her-self back inside. She had rushed to the kitchen and begun to empty shelves before she realized she would need a wagon to do what she proposed. She wanted Matt, and where was he when, this time, she had to have help? But up on the mountain he might not even know what was happening on the river. He no longer worried about her, anyway, just over her children.

She fled outdoors and went racing up the dike to where a few men were at work, moving hurriedly at some task she didn't understand. They were Biddle, Digby and Sander Macabe, who was Molly's husband and the most likely to help her.

None of them paid her any heed until she cried, "Sander Macabe, I'll pay you a hundred dollars if you can get a wagon and—"

They all turned. Macabe said in a harsh voice, "Miz Cowan, get yourself out of here! If this boil gets away from us—!"

"Five hundred!" Libby interrupted.

They ignored her and went on with their job. Libby whirled and rushed again to the building. Steps pounded behind her. Someone grabbed her arm and jerked her around roughly. It was Macabe, his face dark with concern and fury.

"When I said get, I meant get!" he roared. "You pile yourself away from here!"

"Let go of me!"

A hand swung and slapped her hard across the cheek. She gasped at the affront of it, coming from the husband of the woman who worked for her. Yet the hand drew back to strike again.

"If I have to lay you out cold and tote you, I'll do it," he warned. "That dike's sprung a leak. You'd have noticed if you could see past them dollar signs in your eyes. Do you want me to help them try and fix it? Or do I have to lug you out of here?"

"I'm sorry," Libby said weakly. "I'll go."

"I doubt you can get home, though. You make for my place and stay with Molly. It's high enough there I doubt the water'll threaten it. If it does, she's got a level head, and you do what she says. You hear me?"

Libby nodded, ashamed that she had created a problem when they already had trouble to spare. She went inside to get her rainwear while Macabe strode back to the other men. She put on her boots but carried the slicker and hat, for the day was growing fair as any other day of spring. She wasn't sure why she felt compelled to lock the door when she left. Maybe it was habit or, perhaps, it helped keep her believing it would be there for her to unlock again. She was thinking of what Matt had said about her inability to admit defeat. Well, she couldn't, and she would never change.

The men were too absorbed in their efforts to notice when she passed them. Instead of heading for Molly's house as Macabe had advised, she took the footpath for home. Emerging from the first brush, she saw that what had been a pond when she and John came down in the night had become a long and wide lagoon. Her house stood on the far side, still high and dry and only threatened by water on the one side. Smoke still drifted up from the chimney, but she saw no sign of anyone. Escape would have been easy for them and was still, if they hadn't left. She wanted to make sure, now that her hysteria had passed and she was resigned to ruin once more.

She looked to the right to see that the water ran for some distance in that direction. She would have to go around, and it would be a long walk. She retraced her steps, then followed the old road to get over closer to the mountain. The vacated cabins on the lowland drove home her guilt for having thought first of her business. It took an hour to circumvent the floodwater and reach the house.

It was deserted, but Letty had left a note on the center table in the sitting room. "Mamma—we've gone to Amy's. It's high enough there to be out of danger."

A feeling of aversion riffled over Libby's punished nerves. Even in this third crisis of her life, the Biggers name must figure. Well, she wouldn't follow them there. She knew the Biggers cabin stood on high ground. There was rising ground behind it, offering escape should things grow bad enough for the cabin to be threatened. Her own house wasn't immediately endangered. She would stay there until driven out.

Chapter 20

The second leveling of The Cascades was less bellicose but no less thorough than the first, with the Indians and settlers common victims of a river over which they once had fought. The first havoc was wrought at the upper landing, where the abruptly choked channel backed up a ton of water for every tree on the mountains above. Being lower than the Oregon side, the Washington shore took most of the damage. Through a storm-drowned night, frantic men worked to save what they could, some of them drowning in the attempt. In spite of their efforts, the sawmill went out, the cabins, the warehouse on the island, the wharf boat and its mooring wharf, and then the vital portage tracks.

It grew as bad in the six-mile narrows, where savage floodwaters swept away the blockhouse, the cabins around it, isolated Indian camps and the main village, the portage tracks along there, the trestle, and there, also, it claimed lives. The rock banks and reefs lent themselves as nether stones against which the rushing water ground to bits everything swept from the shore for countless miles above, spewing an awesome embolus into the open river below.

With the river wider below the last drowned rapids, the rise was slower but, as it did at the upper landing, the higher Oregon shore crowded the water toward the Washington side. Foot by foot it rose on the dike erected to protect the portage installations until the dike simply

167

burst under an unbearable pressure. And then the un-
leashed water roared over the lowland, united with the
lagoon formed earlier, and shaped a strange new shoreline against the footslope of the mountain.

Libby was given only enough warning to flee from the
house to the nearby knoll where Alister lay buried. There
she turned to see a great lip of water pour in over what
had been the familiar scene of the landing for so many
years. She watched in stunned apathy while a length of
portage track upended and went whipping away to join
the other wreckage cluttering the water. She saw her
building cant while its lower half went under water, then
she watched it cave in and disintegrate. She stared with
vacant eyes while wharf boat, and its contents, snapped
its lines and went careening away. She saw the reaching
folds of water rip out brush and trees. And then cabins,
barns and sheds were dancing crazily and moving away on
the current.

It didn't matter that the knoll on which she stood, supporting herself by the iron fence, had become an island
rising only two or three feet above the water. She turned
her head slowly, at last, to look toward her house. It was
hard to believe that it still stood, although it, too, was an
island with water lapping at its porch. She didn't expect it to stay there. It had only survived the tidal wave
following the collapse of the dike.

She stood with her hands clenched on the railing of the
fence. Which island would survive the longer, the one she
shared with Alister or the one where she had lived so
many years alone with his children? She looked down as
if to speak to him, as she had done so many times, but
her confused mind drifted on. She sank to her knees and
then slumped with shut eyes, her shoulder against the
fence.

She hadn't known of her surrender to exhaustion until
she heard a voice, as if from a great distance. It was urgent yet gentle, a familiar voice.

"Libby—Libby!"

She opened her eyes to discover that she had collapsed
to the ground, that one hand lay in water. She lifted her

head and looked at the grave, for a second under the impression that Alister had called a warning. But someone was shaking her shoulder, and she saw feet and legs and lifted her head to see Matt bent over her.

She managed to say, "How—did you get here?"

"I've got a boat. Where are the children?"

"At—Amy Biggers' cabin."

"All right. Come on."

"No."

She heard his sound of exasperation, then felt herself being lifted and carried. She didn't want to go but didn't fight it. She was too tired. She felt herself lowered into the boat and then was aware of Matt's rowing. She sat up and stared at him with drugged eyes.

"Where were you?" she asked accusingly.

Having asked the question, she lost interest. Disjointedly, she heard Matt say that he had spent most of the night at the upper landing in a hopeless attempt to save the woodyard. It was larger than the one to the lower landing, serving not only the boats but his wood trade in Dalles City. Once it had been swept away, he had helped others there. He hadn't worried about her, for he had supposed her to have sense enough to take the youngsters and head for high ground. As soon as he could get away, he had ridden down, found a boat to row to the house, and from there had seen her on the other island.

She said feebly, "Win?"

"I reckon the *Hassaloe's* tied up and riding it out in Dalles City. They said yesterday it'd be their last trip till things got better. Too much wreckage on the river. And now no place to dock on the Washington side."

"Oh, Matt!" she wailed. "It's all to do over again!"

"You're alive," Matt snapped. "Although God knows what would have happened to you if I hadn't chanced along."

His accusing eyes made her turn her head to see that he was rowing toward the high ground to the west. Quickly, she said, "Where are we going?"

"To Amy's and see about them."

The thought of being taken, broken and exhausted, to the

shelter of the cabin Mose Biggers had thrown together was
loathsome. Yet she was too tired to fight even that. Presently the boat bumped land. They had reached, she realized, the high ground on the west side of the old slough on
Toby's claim.

She must have wrinkled her nose, for Matt said roughly,
"I own it now, and they're gone. Come on."

He helped her out of the boat. She was dizzy and began to
feel hot and cold at the same time. The ground wasn't
steep but seemed so, and pretty soon she realized Matt
had put his arm around her. She felt the pressure of
his hand on her breast, but for some reason it didn't bother
her. They went up across a grassy field, and then she saw
the old Biggers cabin. Intact. The work of Mose Biggers
had outlasted the work of Libby Arlen. She saw figures
emerge from it and start toward them, two young women,
a younger girl and a half-grown boy. They ran forward,
but she could only stumble along with Matt's help.

She didn't look at Amy, saying quickly to Letty,
"Where's John?"

"Why," Letty said, her face suddenly slack, "wasn't he
with you?"

"You—haven't seen him?"

Letty shook her head. "Not since we left to come over
here. He was worried about you, there under that dike.
He went back to bring you. We thought you'd just been
cut off and were together."

"I haven't seen him," Libby said bewilderedly, "since
right after daylight. I—thought he was with you."

There was a black look on Matt's face, but he said
quickly, "I reckon you just missed each other."

"I came around the way he'd have to go," Libby said
in a faint voice. She squeezed her eyes as if that could shut
out the memory of the water crashing through the dike
and in across the lowland. She cried in sudden terror,
"Matt! Find him!"

He nodded and swung to go back down to the boat. Letty
said crisply, "I'm going with you, Matt."

He started to protest, then assented. Libby watched
them hurry down the slope. They belonged together. They

shared, and she was fenced out. And then she felt a hand on her arm and turned to look into Amy's quiet, concerned face.

"Come indoors, Mrs. Cowan," Amy said. "Let me give you some hot coffee."

"Thank you," Libby said stiffly. "But I'll wait out here."

"Please?"

Through some trick of the senses, Libby saw again the face of a small girl, there at Dog River. A girl begging her to eat and refusing to do so herself until Libby had agreed to share a half bowl of the precious gruel. It didn't soften her heart, but it made her follow Amy across the porch and through the door of Mose Biggers' cabin. It made her drop obediently onto a kitchen chair and accept a cup of steaming coffee.

"I'm sure Matt's right," Amy said gently. "You and John just missed each other, somehow. He'll turn up snug and dry."

"If he went around," Libby faltered. "But what if he tried to pick his way across the bottom? In a rush. You know young boys."

Amy looked away so hurriedly, Libby knew this was what she, too, feared. At the house John had seen better than she what was going on elsewhere than the landing. He had already urged her more than once to leave there. When things looked so bad Letty thought they should leave the house and go to Amy's, John would have been beside himself with concern. He wouldn't have gone the long way around for the sake of his own safety.

"Mrs. Cowan!"

Libby felt herself falling from the chair. . . .

She was lying on a clean, comfortable bed in a strange but pleasant room. A blanket covered her, and somebody had pulled off her boots. She was very tired, a little sick, and there was something dreadful at the edge of her waking thoughts that she dared not face. She turned her head, sweeping a fuzzy gaze across the ceiling and down. Matt sat on a chair by the bed, bent forward. He was badly in need of a shave, and his eyes—

She tried to sit up, gasping, "John? Did you find him?"

"Well, Libby—"

"Matt! No!"

She fought to get up and off the bed. He pushed her back. He was stern and gentle, strong and weak all at the same time. She heard him talking, the words like needles slipping into her brain although she tried to keep them out. John had cut across the lowland, as she had feared he would do, but he had got to the landing all right. There, he had been told by the men working on the leak that she had been sent to Molly Macabe's. If only she had been there for him to find. John had looked around, inquiring at other houses standing above flood level. In desperation, at last, he had gone back to the landing, knowing her obsession about her building, and then the dike had burst. Survivors had been able to tell Matt enough for him to put it together.

"Matt, he was a good swimmer. There were floating timbers and logs. Maybe—"

"No, Libby. Don't let yourself hope for that."

She didn't hope, for she knew the river had taken yet another of her loved ones. She lay staring at the ceiling with hot, dry eyes. She knew that if she yielded to it, if she gave way to tears and despair, she would be destroyed herself. And then the blackness clapped down again.

When she next awakened the sickness had left her. There was grief in her heart, but it was as frozen as it had been after Alister was lost. She had been undressed, she discovered, and this time tucked into bed. Turning her head she saw that the chair by the bed was vacant. Matt had gone. Sitting up, she found herself weak and groggy, but she worked her clumsy legs over the edge of the bed. Her clothes? They must have been put away. The cabin was very quiet, not a sound to be heard. She pushed herself onto uncertain feet and crept totteringly to the window and looked out.

Something was very different out there. Then she realized that the river, though still swollen and angry, was back in its banks. The shoreline, while nearly denuded, was much as it had always been. The flat that ran toward the landing was dry. But there was no landing, which told her she hadn't been the victim of a mad dream.

A voice behind her said chidingly, "Mrs. Cowan, you shouldn't be out of bed."

Libby turned to see Amy coming toward her. She said in a cold voice, "The water?"

"You were very sick, Mrs. Cowan, and for a long time. The river crested three days ago and came down fast."

"Where are my children?"

"Mrs. Cowan—" Amy's eyes *were* pretty, and they grew moist. "Some men found John down the river, yesterday. Washed ashore. The funeral had to be in a hurry, and everybody's down there now—where you put Mr. Arlen."

"I want to go there!" Libby cried.

"You can't."

"Then I'll go to my own home!"

Amy shook her head numbly. "It's gone."

The house was a small loss after so much else, but it made the whole too great to bear. "There'll be another, and another business." She lifted her head with flashing eyes. "Twice, now, I've had to start from scratch. I assure you I can do it a third time."

"I know you could and would, Mrs. Cowan. If it could be done."

"Why can't it be done?"

"They won't rebuild our portage road, this time. They'll improve the one on the Oregon side. It came through the flood because it's all on higher ground. Captain Ainsworth thought he should announce that before the portage people who lost their homes built new ones on this side. Just about everything, I guess, will go over there."

Libby made it to the bed before her legs gave way completely. She was too drained to object when Amy tucked her in. Nothing left now but the land for which she came west with Alister. So long—so many weary years ago. What could she do with land, alone, beyond ekeing out a settler's living? Matt might not even acknowledge her right to what she had always thought of as her half of the donation land claim. She felt soft lips touch her cheek.

Something in her eased, and then exhaustion forced her again to sleep.

When she next awakened, a lamp burned in the room, and Matt sat in the chair by the bed. She said with a thick tongue, "Whipped, Matt. Finally."

"But not humbled, from what I hear you said to Amy about starting over."

"Do you want to see me humbled?"

"Not if you can get your eyes open without it." Matt shook his head. "Amy said she told you the north side's finished as a portage. Don't go thinking you can start up an eating-place on the other side. Ainsworth's got big plans. Steel rails and steam locomotives over there. More and better boats that will feed the passengers aboard. I talked to him about it. I knew what you'd figure on."

Libby said with a sigh, "I guess that makes it a clean sweep."

"Not unless you want it to be. You're still my wife."

She turned her head to look at him. "Don't say that, Matt. I never was."

"I mean you are legally." He leaned forward. "If you still want to go away with Margaret and Pip and—Alister, I won't argue. I'll give you your half of everything. But I'd sooner have us all here together. So would your children."

"Oh, Matt. You've loved me dreadfully."

His eyes darkened. "Which is it to be?"

"Will you let me think it over till tomorrow?"

"If you like."

Letty came in with food, and Matt left. Letty looked worn down, for hers had been the direct and immediate grief of seeing John laid to rest that day. She put the tray on Libby's lap, then bent and kissed her brow. "Can you manage? We've spoon-fed you your soup for days."

"I'll manage," Libby said, blinking her eyes. "Don't I always?"

"Yes, Mamma." Letty smiled. "You do."

"Is Matt staying here, too?"

"He's been too worried about you to go back to the woods. He's sleeping in Toby's cabin."

"Have you seen Win?"

Letty nodded. "He's been here every time the *Hassaloe's* been down since it came back into service."

Libby knew how her physical collapse must have upset everyone. Yet it wasn't unpleasant to be fussed and worried over, for a change. She saw that the soup was bean, seasoned with ham. She wondered if Amy was reminding her of that long-ago day when their spirits had touched so briefly. She ate it, and then some custard, while her problem revolved in her mind.

Pip and Margaret came into her room for a while. They were so quiet and left so soon, Libby knew they had been reminded of her need for rest. Matt didn't look in on her again, and she supposed he had gone over to Toby's cabin. Presently Letty came in to settle her for the night. Libby felt too strong to need that but allowed it. Afterward she waited patiently until the last sound died in the cabin, and the crack of light under her door went out. She knew she had been given the one downstairs bedroom, and that the others were sleeping in the loft. She waited for what seemed another hour, then got quietly out of bed.

She found her clothes and the rubber boots she had worn the day she came there, put away in a curtained-off corner of the room. She felt stronger and much steadier and dressed easily. Then she slipped soundlessly from the house. It was a star-bright night, the air was warm, and outdoor motion seemed good after the long shut-in in which her exhausted body and nerves had rested. Toby's cabin, about a quarter-mile away, showed no light. Matt had gone to bed. She was glad of that, for she would have to pass the cabin.

It seemed a long while before she came to the low knoll with its crown of iron fence. The water must have submerged it completely, after Matt took her away from there, but no sign remained of it. Her heart twisted when she came to the fence and saw the fresh earth under flowers that would have come from the neat beds at Amy's cabin.

She had come for counsel and comfort, as she had done so many times, yet all at once she seemed an intruder there. "Alister?" she said, uncertainly and clenched the fence with weak hands. Her eyes refused to leave the fresh flowers and move to the resting place of the one she had addressed.

Alister had no need of her. One of his sons was with him, converted, as she had wanted one of them converted, into his image. Her heart burst with grief, then, for all her lost loved ones. She sank down in the grass and at last wept the tears of a decade. When finally she rose she didn't look at the graves, for no communication was possible. She walked quickly away and, when she had rounded Toby Biggers' slough, came to the cabin that once had been an abomination.

It was fitting, she thought. And then she rapped on the door and waited for Matt to admit her.

Chad Merriman was the pseudonym Giff Cheshire used for his first novel, *Blood on the Sun*, published by Fawcett Gold Medal in 1952. He was born in 1905 on a homestead in Cheshire, Oregon. The county was named for his grandfather who had crossed the plains in 1852 by wagon from Tennessee and the homestead was the same one his grandfather had claimed upon his arrival. Cheshire's early life was colored by the atmosphere of the Old West which in the first decade of the century had not yet been modified by the automobile. He attended public schools in Junction City and, following high school, enlisted in the U.S. Marine Corps and saw duty in Central America. In 1929 he came to the Portland area in Oregon and from 1929 to 1943 worked for the U.S. Corps of Engineers. By 1944, after moving to Beaverton, Oregon, he found he could make a living writing Western and North-Western short fiction for the magazine market and presently stories under the byline Giff Cheshire began appearing in *Lariat Story Magazine*, *Dime Western*, and *North-West Romances*. His short story *Strangers in the Evening* won the Zane Grey Award in 1949. Cheshire's Western fiction was characterized from the beginning by a wider historical panorama of the frontier than just cattle ranching and frequently the settings for his later novels are in his native Oregon. *Thunder on the Mountain* (1960) focuses on Chief Joseph and the Nez Perce war, while *Wenatchee Bend* (1966) and *A Mighty Big River* (1967) are among his best-known titles. However, his Chad Merriman novels for Fawcett Gold Medal remain among his most popular works, notable for their complex characters, expert pacing, and authentic backgrounds.